"Whatever it is, I'll give it to you."

Leon went on silkily. "Just ask me, Alexa. Tell me what you like. Tell me what you want."

He was smiling, the gray of his gaze lit from behind by a satisfaction so intense it was like flames in his eyes.

Alexa's hands clenched into fists as she fought a battle more important than any other in her life. A battle for her life, she thought hazily.

It was so hard to stem the red tide of passion, to quench it with the knowledge that all he wanted of her was the temporary use of her body, whereas she had everything to lose—her pride, her dignity, her heart.

Her voice hard with the effort, the swift color fleeing her skin, she managed to say, "I don't want this."

Robyn Donald lives in northern New Zealand with her husband and children. They love the outdoors and particularly enjoy sailing and stargazing on warm nights. Robyn doesn't remember being taught to read, but rates reading as one of her greatest pleasures, if not a vice. She finds writing intensely rewarding and is continually surprised by the way her characters develop independent lives of their own.

Books by Robyn Donald

ROBYN DONALD

a bitter homecoming

Harlequin Books

TORONTO • NEW YORK • LONDON
AMSTERDAM • PARIS • SYDNEY • HAMBURG
STOCKHOLM • ATHENS • TOKYO • MILAN

Harlequin Presents first edition May 1990
ISBN 0-373-11263-7

Original hardcover edition published in 1989
by Mills & Boon Limited

CHAPTER ONE

THEY were waiting for her as she came out of the customs hall at Auckland Airport; she flinched as a flash went off in her face. The familiar nausea crawled in her stomach but she had learned how to deal with that. No one could see that her skin was clammy, while a straight back and arrogantly held chin gave the lie to her inner trembling.

'Miss Severn—Alexa,' one of the reporters called urgently as she made to walk past them. 'Did you know that Samuel Darcy tried to commit suicide after you left England?'

Cameras recorded her gasp and the momentary stark shock in her expression. However, it vanished immediately, replaced by a hauteur that hardened her beautiful face into a mask. Her mouth tightened and she said nothing.

They tried again. 'He shot himself.'

And waited. It was a technique she knew well. An international one, she thought wearily, then pushed to the back of her mind memories of their counterparts in London. They were standing in a solid wall in front of her, partly blocking her off from the other people in the concourse, but she was taller than most of them and over their heads she sensed the curious looks, the sudden recognition and the avid whisperings. What had made her assume that New Zealand would be a refuge?

'Excuse me,' she said firmly and pushed on through, her suitcase held protectively in front of her. They eased

back. Not exactly the same as their English counterparts, she decided with grim resignation. Not quite so
bloodthirsty.

'What are you going to do now you're back in New
Zealand?'

'Have you a job to go to here?'

'Why did Samuel Darcy try to kill himself? His wife
blames you. Any comment?'

'No comment.' Her voice was hard and clear and cold,
a faint English accent overlying the basic New Zealand
inflection and intonation.

Her brilliant blue eyes flat and opaque, she strode out
through the doors to the taxi that waited for her. The
reporters followed, asking questions, demanding
answers, their voices blending in a cacophony of questions until the slam of the door cut them off. The driver
was clearly curious, but courtesy forbade him to show
it.

'The Sheraton,' she said, exhausted, yet conscious that
she had to hold out until she reached the sanctuary of
her hotel room. Only then could she allow herself to be
shocked by Samuel's suicide attempt. Closing her eyes,
she let an image of the island fill her mind, dwelling
lovingly on the remembered hills and beaches, the dear,
familiar contours of headlands and sea—the only place,
she thought with a flash of shaming self-pity, where she
had been really happy.

A fool's paradise, because even as a child she had
known that her mother hated the place. It was under-
standable. What had possessed a sophisticated woman
from London to think that she could ever be happy living
on a sheep and cattle station some miles off the northern
coast of New Zealand?

She had tried. Mary Severn had really loved the man she had married, but by the time Alexa was fifteen it was all over. Mary left for the brighter lights of London, and her husband sold the island and took his broken heart and his bitterness to another station, miles up a secondary road in the high volcanic plateau at the centre of the North Island. But he had kept a small patch of his ancestral land at Honeymoon Bay, a little house that stood on four acres of ground. It was rarely visited. His second wife didn't like anything that reminded him of that first marriage. Which was why Alexa was headed there now, and not to her father.

At the hotel she made a call to her greatest friend, only to be told by the housekeeper that Cathy and Jake and their two children were away in South America. Alexa pushed a hand through thick black hair and closed her eyes. More than anything she had wanted to talk to Cathy.

Biting her lip, she dialled through to the operator. The island was connected to one of the very few manual exchanges left in the country. However, the pleasant woman who took her call gave no indication that she recognised Alexa's voice, merely putting her through to the manager of the station. When the call was answered, she didn't recognise the voice, but it had been some years since she had spoken to anyone from the island.

'Hello. Is that the homestead on Severn Island?' Her normally warm tones sounded cold, brusque with control, but she couldn't help that. The strain of the last few months was showing.

'Yes,' he responded crisply.

She said, 'That is Ted Oakes?'

'No. Ted left six months ago.'

She caught back a surprised exclamation. On the verge of giving him her name, she paused. Better not. It wasn't likely that he would tell the Press, but you never knew who was listening. 'I—see. I'm the daughter of the man who owns Honeymoon Bay. I'm coming up to the island tomorrow and I wondered if I could hitch a ride back on the barge.'

He said curtly, 'No.'

After an astounded moment Alexa said, 'I see,' and found tears in her eyes. She ironed out a husky note in her voice and finished stupidly, 'Never mind, it's all right.'

But the new manager hadn't finished. In a voice that was deep and cool and abrupt he went on, 'We can't, of course, stop you from staying on your land. But from now on, if you step over the boundary it will be considered that you are trespassing, and you will be treated as such.'

The last sentence was delivered with a relish that stunned Alexa. She was silent for so long that he had time to say, 'Do I make myself clear?'

Then she gathered her wits about her enough to make some sort of reply. 'Yes,' she said, vaguely, and he hung up, leaving her standing there with the receiver pressed to her ear while the silent tears slipped down her cheeks.

She put the receiver down and moved with considerably less than her usual grace across the room, switching on the television set. The continuity announcer smiled and welcomed her to a comedy. With a shudder Alexa switched it off. She had been staring at the empty screen for some minutes before she realised that he had been sitting in front of a Christmas tree.

Alexa hadn't even realised. Trapped by the circus she had allowed to be made of her life, she had forgotten that it was almost Christmas Day.

Nostalgia brought more tears to her eyes, tears she scrubbed at angrily. It had to be stress, but she was crying far too easily nowadays. Surely a holiday on the island would ease the tension that pulled through her body like wires?

After a night spent in the embrace of a sleeping pill she hired a car and began the long drive up the thin spine of Northland to the small settlement of Hogarth. Originally she had intended to fly, but her experience at the airport made her wary. She chose a car with tinted windows and tied a scarf around her head in an attempt to disguise herself, as well as donning a large pair of dark glasses. Hackneyed, but it worked. No one accosted her all day.

The road north brought an uplifting of her spirits, a faint intimation that life might yet have some joy for her. Stopping in one of the small villages on the way she bought two enormous cartons of groceries and a selection of paperbacks, making sure that one was a book of crossword puzzles.

Thus armed for anything she drove on through a day made wearisome by heat and crowded roads and, for the last twenty miles, a narrow gravel track that had her frowning as she peered through the clouds of dust. Occasionally she ran a hand across the tense muscles at the back of her neck. An incipient headache lurked, waiting for her to lose concentration so that it could pounce. She hoped that she'd be on the island before it made life impossible for her. Her doctor had said that they were caused by tension; whatever, when one struck she was incapable of anything beyond lying in bed in a darkened room waiting for it to leave in its own good time.

When she had lived on the island Hogarth had been nothing more than a general store and a hall, a church and a sports ground and a primary school above the bay. In the summer people came to stay at the camping ground and swim from the long stretch of pale sand that ended in an abrupt hill carved into the terraces that had defended it in the days when it was a famous fighting *pa*, or Maori settlement. Descendants of those Maoris still lived in the area, but instead of fighting they farmed their ancestral lands and fished from small numbered fishing boats.

Alexa had never really realised that it was her home, her heart's resting place. Since Whangarei she had felt the pure singing of anticipation, a siren call that had never entirely faded, not in all the long years she had spent away. Pulling off the road above the bay, she got out and looked down over a wild tangle of trees and scrub punctuated by the spiralling whorls of tree ferns. Below, the small town straggled along the beach. It should have been raw, even ugly, but the beauty of its setting transcended the small box-like houses, each one set in its own garden, gay now with subtropical shrubs.

There were a few new houses, a small block of shops. Beyond them the road wandered on to the jetty beneath the *pa*. The island barge rocked beside it, ugly and serviceable. Great pohutukawa trees blazed scarlet and crimson all around the coast, spreading wide over the flat areas, clinging to the cliffs. New Zealand's Christmas tree, the symbol of summer.

Far enough out to sea to be in a different universe was the island, shaped like a sleeping lion, the hills already tawny although it was only a month into summer. The rhythms of a childhood spent on the land asserted themselves in Alexa. The island had always been prone to drought, and it looked as though a bargeload of cattle had been sent across to the mainland to ease the pressure on the pastures.

Slowly, her face shuttered, she turned the ignition on and drove down the narrow, hairpin bends to the village.

She dropped the car off at the garage, accepting the proprietor's offer to leave her parcels there until she was ready to go.

'Is there anyone who might take me across to Severn Island?' she asked.

He looked a little surprised. 'Well, the barge is in, but I heard they're not going back until late; they're meeting the carrier from Whangarei. One of the fishermen might do it—try Tom Hoskings. He runs a sort of water-taxi affair when there's any call for it. Second house on the left towards the jetty. Can't miss it—he's got his crayfish pots on the lawn.'

After thanking him she walked carefully down the rough road towards the wharf, wondering rather desperately how she was going to get across to the island if Tom Hoskings wasn't prepared to take her across. It had been stupid to come up without making arrangements, but she had been intent only on reaching sanctuary, had fled twelve thousand miles to get there, and she wasn't going to be put off by the arrogant rudeness of the manager last night.

Deep in thought, she heard her name called. Her first impulse was to flee, but, stiffening her back, she met the stare of the man who was sauntering along towards her.

'It is Alexa Severn, isn't it?' He looked her over, cockily confident.

'Yes.'

'Remember me?' He was level with her now, grinning in a way that made her faintly uneasy. Or perhaps it was the headache. A chill wave ran over her skin as the familiar rhythm began to beat behind her eyes. 'We were in the same class together at school.'

She hated people who teased by asking unanswerable questions, but a door popped open in her memory and she said, 'Sean Pearson.'

Shoving his hands into his pockets, he grinned again. 'Yeah, that's right.'

He had grown up to be a very attractive man, lean and hard-bitten, an inch or so taller than she was. Unfortunately, he was eyeing her in a way she had endured too often since she had grown to be the possessor of a long, well-shaped body and a face that followed most norms for beauty.

Time to freeze him off. Her head lifted. In a cool, detached little voice she said, 'Nice to see you again, Sean.'

He jerked his head at the outline of the island on the horizon. 'Heading for home?'

'Yes.' Her head was thumping, and even through the smoked lenses of her sunglasses the sun hurt her eyes.

He said slowly, 'Hear you're not allowed across on the barge.'

It had been her mother's opinion, still held, that everyone in New Zealand was either related to everyone else or knew of them. And, as a bitter corollary, that everyone knew what everyone else was doing all the time. It was hardly unusual in a country of only three million people.

Alexa's lovely mouth sketched a smile. 'Your sources of information are accurate.'

He grinned again, letting his eyes wander over her once more in a manner she would have found offensive if she hadn't been feeling so wretched. It occurred to her that she should have breakfasted on a little more than a cup of strong black coffee.

'Well, I work there and the boss didn't make any bones about it. Told us all that you weren't welcome anywhere on the place. How're you going to get across?'

She shrugged, then wished she hadn't as her head stepped up its thumping. Through it she said, 'I'll find someone to take me across. The man at the garage said Tom Hoskings...'

He was shaking his head. 'He's away on holiday. You can come back with me, if you like.'

'No,' she said. 'I don't want to lose you your job.'

He grinned, watching her from beneath pale lashes. In his voice there was arrogance and a certain insolence, but his next words made it clear that they were not directed at her. 'The boss might think he's got us all where he wants us, but I can do what I want in my own boat, on my day off. What sort of joker would I be if I didn't lend a hand to an old schoolfriend?'

Alexa hesitated, but the sudden wave of nausea that swept over her convinced her. She gave him a pale smile and said, 'Thank you. If you're sure it won't cause you any trouble.'

'Guarantee it. He's not there today, anyway.' As if angry with himself for letting this out, he said, 'You go and get into the boat. It's the blue and white one down at the jetty. *The Dove.* Go into the cabin and sit down. You don't look too good. Is that all you're taking with you?'

'No, the rest of my luggage is at the garage,' she said. 'I'll go and get it.'

'No need, I'll pick it up.'

'Thank you.'

He looked at her shrewdly. 'A little fresh air'll put some colour in your cheeks.'

The boat was large and, as she saw when she made her way into the cabin, luxurious. Too far gone to do more than wonder how Sean Pearson had raised the money to buy a sleek expensive toy like this, Alexa sank down on to a long banquette with a sigh of relief that seemed to come from the depths of her being.

Her head tipped back. She closed her eyes for a moment's blessed peace, and within a few seconds was sound asleep.

She didn't hear Sean Pearson come back on board, didn't see him pause in the doorway and look down at her, didn't even hear the throaty purr of the great engines beneath her. In fact, she was so deeply asleep that the sound of a fresh set of engines only just penetrated through to her exhausted brain. Frowning, she stirred, and muttered, and only very gradually came up through the unknown waters of sleep to surface at last. Her eyes opened and she stared blankly all around, blinking slowly. Her head throbbed, but much more gently than it had before.

Remembrance came swiftly. Staggering a little, she got to her feet and went up the steps into the cockpit. The new noise seemed to come from above. Her forehead pleated as she tried to place it.

Of course—a helicopter! And one flown too damned close, from the sound of it.

A roar from the man at the wheel whipped her head around. 'Get below!'

So imperative was his tone that she found herself halfway down the steps before she had had time to think.

But when she did, she realised that if that helicopter held the man Sean called the boss, then naturally he wouldn't want him to see his contraband passenger.

Worried in case he had been lying when he had boasted that he couldn't be held accountable for helping her, she waited until the sound of the helicopter died away before going up into the cockpit once more.

'Was that your employer?' she asked diffidently.

He shrugged, shooting her a hard look. 'Yeah. Nosy b-beggar came over to see what I was doing.'

Alexa didn't attempt to hide her concern. 'I do hope you're not going to get into trouble. I shouldn't have come with you...'

'Listen, I'm not scared of Leon Venetos. He thinks he's the big man, but I——'

'Leon Venetos?' She stared at him blankly. 'Is he—does Leon Venetos own the island now?'

He looked sullen and truculent at the same time. Alexa recalled suddenly that he was the only son in a family of doting sisters. 'Didn't you know he's bought the island? Had it for two years now.'

'No,' she said slowly. 'No. I didn't know.'

'He's been pouring money into it like water. I tell you, if I had half the money that's been spent on this place I'd be a rich man. And not even for sensible reasons, either. I mean, if it's to increase productivity, fair enough. But he's planted trees all over the hills; not pines, that he can cut in thirty years and make a profit on, but natives, for heaven's sake. They'll have to be watered every summer for bloody years. *Taraire* and *puriri* and *rimu*, none of them ready to cut until well after we're all dead and gone. He's crazy. Every winter students come up to plant more and more on the hills—in a few years there'll only be half the area in grass that there is now.'

It was clearly a familiar plaint, delivered frequently. Ignoring it for the moment Alexa asked, 'Did I speak to him last night?'

'Yeah.' He looked across at her, half smiling. 'Unpleasant sod, isn't he.'

Colour invaded her cheeks, indignation and a familiar shame mixed. 'He certainly made himself clear.'

In her abortive career as a finance expert in London she had heard of the Venetos Corporation and the man who headed it, but had never met him. He did not like publicity and, because he had the sort of power that went with huge wealth and influence, he was able to enforce his likes and dislikes on the often unwilling media. Sam used to talk of him with awe. Brilliant, charismatic and totally ruthless, the man who had sprung from anonymity in New Zealand to eminence on the world stage had been a man her mentor envied and tried to emulate.

Showing a streak of ruthlessness that might have saved her had she managed to use it in her career, she pushed all thoughts of Sam away. Time enough to worry about him when she was safe on the island.

'Well,' she said uneasily, 'I don't intend to be seeing him, so I'm not going to worry about his paranoia.'

Sean shrugged. 'Yeah, well, he's not likely to be here for long.'

'Does he spend much time on the island? It seems a long way from the power centres of the world.'

'He comes and goes. He doesn't exactly encourage interest in his movements. He doesn't socialise at all, although he sometimes brings a girlfriend to keep his bed warm.' His voice thickened, became coloured with envy. 'There's one there now. Lady Somebody-or-other.

He has great taste. As for distance, he's got the home-stead set up with an electronics room that'd do justice to the foreign exchange room of a bank. Must have cost him bloody millions to set it up. Still, millions is one thing he's got plenty of.'

Alexa was alarmed to discover that she didn't like Sean very much. She didn't like the over-familiar way his eyes rested on her breasts and hips, she didn't like the smile that sat so curiously on his lips, and she didn't like the way he spoke of his employer. Leon Venetos sounded a swine, but he was owed some loyalty, surely?

Still, she had accepted help from Sean, and she was going to have to make the best of it. She wasn't afraid, just wary. If the worst came to the worst, she knew several tricks that would give him severe pain in various portions of his anatomy and make him think twice before trying anything again.

She changed the subject. 'How long is it since anyone stayed at the bach?'

'Hell, I don't know.'

He squinted ahead at the island, which was growing larger by slow, unremarkable increments. The bold outline had lost its resemblance to a lion, resolving into hills and gullies, the parched pasture gleaming golden and rufous against a brazen sky. Sean's wide hand pushed his cap back into an even jauntier position. She noted that the nails were ingrained with what seemed to be oil, and concluded that he was employed in some capacity to do with engines.

He saw her look at him, and smiled, and she looked away, angry for giving him the opening. There was a note of satisfaction in his voice as he said, 'Must be three, four years, I'd say, since anyone was there. They were a honeymoon couple. Friends of your father's.'

Alexa made a small grimace. 'I hope it's in a reasonable state.'

'Should be. Nothing much can go wrong in that length of time. Ted Oakes used to keep an eye on it until he retired. Don't know if the new man does.'

She said in her most matter-of-fact tone. 'The place was built to be easy to look after. I remember my mother chose ceramic tiles for the floors and the kitchen and bathroom for that reason. I'll probably have to wash the place free of daddy-long-legs and clean the salt off the windows, but I doubt if there'll be much else to do.'

'I hope not.' He cast another glance her way, eyeing her slyly. 'Be a pity to waste the summer scrubbing and cleaning. You should be out getting a tan on that beautiful skin.'

Alexa pretended not to hear that unwelcome observation and moved away to look over the side towards the island.

Homestead Bay was a crescent of silver backed by buildings among the sombre shelter of *totara* trees. A little above the bay the two-storeyed homestead gleamed white. Dormer windows pierced the *kauri* shingles on the roof. Without thinking, Alexa counted off the three workers' cottages, solid and bigger than their name implied, the wool-shed and all the other buildings that were necessary on a place so far from workshop and store.

Something eased, relaxed into calmness deep inside her. The wind of their motion tossed her hair about her face in skeins of black silk, so she pulled out her scarf from the pocket of her jacket and tied it over her head. The salt air smelt delicious, cool and tangy. She took long slow breaths and, for the first time in centuries, she smiled.

As if she had summoned them, a school of dolphins surged and swam and leaped clear out of the water in pure joy and harmony. Still smiling, she leaned out to watch them. For a moment it seemed as though they might come and escort the vessel, but they turned out towards the open sea, and Alexa sighed.

Apollo's darlings, she thought, the children of the sea. How like a Mediterranean island this was, and how different...

She stayed where she was while Homestead Bay slid behind them, then a headland of red rocks with a clashing scarlet coverlet of pohutukawa trees, and beyond that Honeymoon Bay, secret and sheltered behind a barrier of islets and rocks, the long reef that shielded it from the worst excesses of the open sea clawing out towards the mainland. Sean took the big launch skilfully in through the narrow channel, cut the engine, and in the abrupt silence let the anchor down with a sharp rattle, while Alexa looked shorewards in dismay.

The four acres of land that her father had kept was newly fenced off by a chain fence; the grass that used to be eaten short by sheep was now lank and unkempt, as were the fruit trees and the few others that had survived years of neglect. Almost hidden in the tangle was the small cottage that was the only thing Alexa could call her home in all the world. A ruin and a wreck of dreams, she thought cynically. And then, well, so what? It's more than many people ever have.

Bending a little, she pulled the painter of the small dinghy that had trailed behind them all the way from the mainland. It came smoothly up to the bigger craft, and Sean dumped her suitcase and the boxes of supplies into it.

'In you get,' he said. She stumbled a little, and he grinned. 'You used to be more at home in boats than you were in cars when you were a kid. Has your life in the jet set made you forget how the peasants live?'

'New Zealand,' she said repressively, 'has never had peasants. And no, I haven't forgotten. It's just a while since I had anything to do with boats.'

He unfastened the painter, then got lithely in and unshipped the oars. As he rowed in, Alexa was uneasily aware that beneath his heavy lids his gaze never left her, drifting from her face to her breasts and back again. It was a bold scrutiny, one he wasn't attempting to hide. She realised that she had been stupid to allow her headache to lure her into what seemed more and more likely to be a trap.

Alexa resigned herself to a tussle, recriminations when he realised that she wasn't going to respond, and then more or less friendly relations. She knew the type. There were men like Sean all over the world, and mostly they didn't worry about trying too hard. Possessed of a natural virility and a healthy sense of their own worth, they didn't see the sense in wasting time pursuing one woman when there were always others willing and ready for their brand of somewhat soulless magnetism.

He didn't seem to be the sort of man who would indulge in rape; he looked to be the local sexually successful Romeo. He would have no hesitation in pressing his demands on any woman who seemed receptive, but if she clearly wasn't enthusiastic, he'd go on to more likely prospects.

When the soft scrunch of sand beneath the dinghy signalled their arrival she jumped out and pulled it a little further up the beach, turning her head away when

Sean said with elaborate casualness, 'Hell, it's hot, isn't it? I'll take off my shirt.'

She stooped and picked up her suitcase, walking a little swiftly up the soft, white sand towards the chain fence. Anger spurted up through her wariness as she saw a sign nailed to one of the supports of the only gate in it; 'Private Property', it warned. 'Keep Out'.

'Making sure you get the message.' Sean's voice was an intrusion.

She said bitterly, 'He's not exactly subtle, your boss, is he? Especially as I have riparian rights and the beach belongs to me down to the mean low-water mark.'

'To you? Thought it was your father's.'

Her father had given it to her as a twenty-first birthday present, but she could see no reason why she should tell him that.

Secretly she was appalled at the general air of neglect, but she wasn't going to show it. Striding confidently through the gate, she headed towards the wide veranda, dumping the case on to the quarry tiles beneath the pergola. She turned, ignoring the speculative gleam in his eyes. 'I'll come with you to get the rest of the stuff.'

'Might as well check the place,' he said easily. 'You unlock and I'll bring up the other boxes.'

He turned away before she could protest and swaggered across the long wiry grass that had once been a lawn. Fishing for the key in her bag, Alexa watched the sun play on the burnished muscles of his shoulders and frowned, fighting the feeling that somehow the initiative had been taken away from her. The dull throbbing behind her eyes began to pick up speed.

Slowly she unlocked and stepped inside, her eyes taking quite some time to adjust to the dimness there after the glare of the sunlight. With dilated eyes she looked around, taking in the detritus of the last four years.

Surprisingly, it wasn't too bad. Oh, it was dusty, and grubby, but it wouldn't take her long to clean it up. She heard Sean come in and moved across the quarry tiles towards the kitchen at the back of the room, separated from the huge sitting and dining area only by a half-wall.

He was carrying both remaining boxes, the corded muscles in his arms standing out. He looked bigger than she had realised, and as she moved across the room he passed her with a sideways smile that set every alarm bell in her brain jingling. She thought distractedly that she could smell the anticipation in him, a kind of musky masculine scent that set her nerves on edge.

Coolly, her armour firmly in place, she walked across to the windows and pulled the curtains back, letting in light. A quick flick of her wrist opened the wide doors, and the stale, thick air was dispelled by the salt tang. She could feel his eyes on her; the hair on the back of her neck lifted, and at last she had to turn and face him.

He was smiling as he came across the room, and she felt that first real pang of fear like a kick in the stomach. Quickly, before it had time to flower into panic, she said, 'Thank you very much for bringing me across. I hope you don't get into any sort of trouble...'

'It'll be worth it,' he said in a meaningful tone. 'I'm sure you can make it worthwhile for me. You must have learned a lot since you left this place.'

She put up her hand in a gesture that should have stopped him, but even as her expression mirrored her distaste he reached out and grabbed her. Through her teeth she said, 'And what gives you the idea that you can just grab?'

He laughed. 'Call it payment. You're used to being paid for sleeping with people, aren't you? Well, I've paid. I brought you across here. Now I want to collect. And it had better be good.'

With the mark of her open hand on his cheek, he stared into her furious face and laughed, her resistance exciting him. Those strong arms tightened, and she was brought against his body which was already, she realised with dismay, considerably aroused.

'According to the papers you've been sleeping mostly with older men,' he said, letting her feel his strength as he held her against him. His voice was thick, his eyes glittering; a dark stain lay across his skin. 'Why not give yourself a treat and try someone with the stamina to match you? You might find you enjoy having sex with someone around your age for a change.'

She said calmly, 'If you let me go we'll forget about this.'

Even as she said it she knew it was no good. Clearly he had been anticipating this all the way across, and such was his conceit that it didn't occur to him that she was doing anything more than being coy.

He laughed and bent his head and kissed her, forcing her mouth open in a way that made her gag. He lifted his head and said roughly, 'What the hell——?' and she brought her hands up, the palms cupped, and slammed them over his ears, not too hard because she didn't want to burst his eardrums.

It hurt. He swore and gave an involuntary stagger back, his face darkening. She said steadily, 'Sean, I could kill you if I wanted to.'

'Only if I let you, you bitch.'

He began to lurch towards her. Alexa had time to spring into a self-defence posture when the light through the windows was interrupted and a crisp, savage voice cracked, 'What the hell is going on here?'

Sean's reaction would have been ludicrous if it hadn't been so startling. All of his bravado was shown up for the brittle thing it was. He went white and straightened up, his eyes fixed on to the man who had just stepped in through the door as though he was the devil incarnate.

'Well?'

Alexa's arms came down to her side. She turned and followed Sean's gaze. The man who had just entered was big; that much she had seen in the first incredulous glance. But now she saw much more. He had blond hair, the colour of the sun on the sand, with auburn streaks through it, yet he was tanned with the kind of colour that denoted an olive skin. And his eyes were dark, as were his lashes and brows, so that he was a mixture of dark and fair, sunlight and ebony.

However, after her first stunned glance, his colouring made no impact. What kept her silent and afraid was the astonishing beauty of his face, the blazing, potent beauty of Lucifer, fierce and bold and bright, and the danger that lay behind the superficial harmony of feature and colouring. Alexa had seen many handsome men. Her closest friend, Cathy, was married to one who had the ability to make women forget their manners and stare, but she had never been pierced to the heart by the sight of a man as she was now.

He said impatiently, 'Are you Alexa Severn?'

Slowly, reluctantly, the sirens that had been singing their perilous song in her brain quietened. Danger of a different sort spoke to her. Cautiously, her voice so soft that it barely disturbed the dusky silence, she said, 'I— I am staying here. Who are you?'

'I, too, am staying here.' The mockery was acerbic. 'No, not in this house. At the homestead.'

She groped frantically for caution, poise, and managed to say almost calmly, 'I didn't hear you come.'

'I'm sorry I startled you.' It was said with hard sarcasm, and she didn't like the way those dark eyes raked across her face and body.

Very slowly, like a small animal in danger, she eased herself away from him, her lashes hiding the confusion and fear in her eyes.

'So you are Alexa Severn,' he said far too smoothly. They had been speaking as if Sean was no longer there, but now those dark eyes imprisoned him. 'Take the launch back to the homestead,' he ordered without expression, 'and wait for me there.'

Sean looked very young, his aggression shown up for pure bravado. Ignoring Alexa, he said, 'I can explain——'

'You had better be able to. Now go.'

And Sean left them as if the devil had been after him. Had Alexa not been so tense, she might have found something amusing in the speed of his departure.

'Did you know that Sam Darcy tried to kill himself?'

Through her astonishment Alexa recognised the voice that had been so rude on the telephone the night before.

'Well?' he demanded, a savage sarcasm colouring the deep tones with their hint of some other accent behind the educated New Zealand inflection.

Perhaps it was the culmination of the past horrible months, perhaps merely exhaustion mixed with jet lag, but Alexa, who prided herself on her composure, was unable to do more than stare at him. Pain was like a jagged spear through her body. 'Yes,' she said tonelessly, aware that this man had judged her. And there was no mercy in him.

He was watching her, his expression as cold as that of a snake before it strikes. 'It doesn't worry you? You don't feel any desire to rush back to your lover, to give him some reason to live?'

All emotion fled from her face. Her features hardened, became blank and closed; the light left her eyes, so that they were opaque blue enamel, bright of colour but empty.

'No.'

He smiled, far from pleasantly. 'I see. I came over to see what sort of woman had made Sam forget that he had a wife and children. I must say, I admire his taste.' His gaze ran the length of her body, insolently assessing, blatant with contempt. It was infinitely more humiliating than Sean's lustful survey.

White to the lips, Alexa held her head so high that her neck ached. She said nothing.

After that utterly shaming survey of her breasts and waist, the feminine curve of hips, the long, sleek line of her thighs beneath the cotton slacks, he resumed, 'However, I do not admire a man who puts his mistress in a position of responsibility in his firm and then pushes her up through the ranks until the scandal is notorious and all the world, as well as his wife, gets to hear of it. Still less do I admire a woman who, when her name has become a byword for sleeping her way up the ladder, flees from the besotted fool and leaves him so shattered that the only thing he can think of to do is try to kill himself.'

Alexa looked at him but she didn't see the hard contemptuous face, or the magnificent bone structure, did not even register the overwhelming presence of the man.

She had learned that the only way to deal with those intent on tormenting her was to retreat to somewhere deep inside where no one could reach her.

Cold and proud, flat eyes unwinking in a still white face, her mouth a straight line, chin level; no, he couldn't see beyond the mask. The silence stretched between them, unrelenting, sizzling with unspoken thoughts. From outside came the monotonous yapping of a pied stilt. She remembered that a pair used to nest in the swamp beside the creek and wondered stupidly if they were the same birds, or were they long since dead?

'No answer, Miss Severn? No justifications, no remorse.'

'I don't have to justify myself to you, whoever you are,' she said stonily.

He laughed softly. 'I am Leon Venetos. As you know. And no, you don't have to justify yourself. You couldn't do it, so it would be a waste of time to try. However, let me warn you that I am less susceptible than your previous lovers, much less so than poor Sean.'

'*Poor Sean,*' she said softly, 'was all set to rape me.'

'Not from where I saw it. You looked as though you were well able to look after yourself. But I suppose women of your profession need to be. It was a little unfair, however, to persuade him to bring you across in my launch, a ploy that you must have realised would lose him his job, and then refuse to pay him the reward you clearly offered him. No wonder Sam Darcy tried to kill himself.'

If she had learned anything in these last months it was that protesting her innocence did no good at all. Sickened though she was by his attack, she did nothing more than shrug her shoulders.

'Nevertheless,' she said remotely, 'I'm glad you turned up when you did. Even though you must take the prize for jumping to conclusions. Thank you.'

She turned and walked across to the kitchen, blindly seeking to put as much distance between them as she could. The deep throbbing of the launch's engines barely impinged. Clumsily, ignoring the man who watched her, she began to unpack the groceries she had bought. Just the bare essentials for a camping holiday; most of her provisions were freeze-dried or tinned, with vegetables wrapped in newspaper.

Her hands trembled a little as she freed them, then stilled. What little colour there was left in her skin vanished, and she bit back a gasp of pain, for her own face looked out at her from the page.

Above it the headlines screamed 'Woman in Centre of Scandal Arrives Home'. Beneath it was a paragraph long on innuendo, short on facts. 'Alexa Severn, New Zealand-born executive of Smithers and Darcy, Merchant Bankers of London, arriving at Auckland International Airport late last night. Miss Severn has been named as co-respondent in a sexual and financial scandal extending to some of the biggest names in British finance.'

The photograph gave her features a hardbitten, sullen cast. She looked like everyone's conception of a woman who had slept her way to a position of influence and power.

Leon Venetos's reluctant voice asking her if she was all right finally cut through the mantle of pain. She lifted her head to stare at him, and saw that he was coming towards her. Some pitiful remnant of pride made her hands move to crumple the sheets of newspaper, but he had seen. His brows drew together as he took it from her and spread it out so that he could read it.

Her head thumping, sick to her stomach, she waited, only willpower keeping her erect. After all the trauma of the past months it seemed amazing that it should take a man she had never met before to bring home to her just how degraded she felt.

'You must have seen worse,' he said abruptly.

She was too tired to lie. 'Not here.' In spite of her courage, her voice wobbled.

He looked at her. 'I see. But you haven't been a New Zealander for some years. Didn't you go to Harvard?'

How did he know that? Going to Harvard had been part of her need to meet her mother's expectations, although she hadn't realised it at the time. She had abandoned her long-held ambitions to specialise in pure mathematics and taken a graduate managerial course, and from there she had made her way up the corporate ladder, helped by an uncanny intuition about the money market, until she had arrived at London, and Smithers and Darcy, Merchant Bankers.

And from thence, she thought with bitter irony, to the front pages of every scandal sheet in the world.

She could feel his eyes on her, sharp and cold and appraising, and something inside her, hitherto inviolate, shattered. A cold tide of sweat stood out on her skin; she gave a moan and fled into the bathroom.

The next few minutes were profoundly unpleasant, but their very nastiness made it possible for her to forget the man who had made her realise that she could never go back. When she had finished, and was washing her face in the stale, lukewarm water that was all that came from the tap, he came in.

She knew what she looked like. Migraines were not noted for adding to one's attractions, and the inevitable nausea and its aftermath had left her white and shaking.

And she did not want Leon Venetos watching her. But before she could speak he said curtly, 'What is the matter with you? Are you pregnant?'

'Migraine.' She couldn't even summon any outrage.

'I see.' His brows were drawn together in a frown. He watched her as she dried her face slowly, because the drag of the towel hurt her super-sensitive skin, and then he said with every appearance of reluctance, 'Well, you can't stay here. I'll take you home.'

She should have protested. She should have told him to go to hell. She looked at him and through the haze of pain she saw something that told her she was safe, and she gave in. Just this once, she promised herself. And only because she couldn't get the place ready to live in in this state.

CHAPTER TWO

SHE woke the next morning in the room that had once been hers. Her eyes opened on to the view she had loved as a child, and for long moments she lay quietly, pretending that she was still at home, that the intervening years with their slow remorseless erosion of childhood's trust and joy had never happened.

Experimentally she moved her head, delighted to find that the pain had gone. She felt a little stiff, a little light-headed, but perfectly well and whole, as if yesterday's headache had been only a figment of her imagination. Slowly she looked around the room. It was a far cry from the friendly shabbiness that had been its main attribute when she slept there. She was lying in a French cherrywood bed, the warm tones of the wood repeated in a superb dressing table. Instead of wallpaper the walls were covered with a wash in a fascinating creamy apricot tint that looked like the interior of a shell, the colour of all the sunrises she had ever seen.

White cotton curtains striped in a thin pale apricot line billowed from the ceiling to the floor, hiding french windows that were wide open to let in the dawn. Beyond them the boards of the veranda that went around two sides of the first and second storeys of the house gleamed warmly. Alexa rose from the bed, and almost tiptoed out into the morning. The white classic railings, simple and restrained as only the Georgians knew how to make them, were wet with dew. She breathed in deeply and rested her hands on to the wood, listening with delight to a cock crowing somewhere behind the house.

The garden had been reworked and was now Mediterranean in appearance, the tall palm trees with their rough trunks reaching up through a delightful shrubbery of oleanders and daisies and flax, roses and ginger and fuchsias, with native shrubs and trees used for accent and beauty.

Beyond the hedge was the sea, still and hazy, the blue of an angel's wing. A gull flew up into the rising sun, transformed from his everyday livery into a magical golden bird. Phoenix rising, she thought, as she turned to go back in. She did not want anyone to catch her clad only in the silken pyjamas she had packed in that last frantic hurry to get away from London.

She was too late. Leon Venetos stood in the doorway of the next room, eyeing her with a coolly impersonal interest that she found far more offensive than Sean Pearson's hot desire had been. He wore a pair of trousers and nothing else, and he looked virile and over-powering, his shoulders wide and tanned, fine scrolls of hair curling across his chest to form a line snaking down beyond the waistband of his jeans.

'Good morning,' she said tonelessly, as she walked back across the boards of the veranda, her toes curling under that cool scrutiny. Something strange was happening in the region of her stomach.

'Good morning. How is your head?'

She was seized by an unnerving sensation, one she had never experienced before, as though somehow her skin had become sensitised. The silk flowed smoothly, erotically, over her body, setting tiny nerve impulses afire; she *felt* the length of her legs, the sleek thoroughbred lines of her limbs, the way her hair grew from her head and fell smoothly around her shoulders, every small sensation in her skin and bones. And when she drew a deep, impeded breath the air tasted of fire and honey in her mouth.

It was the man who watched her who was doing it. His cool gaze set something free, something that she had not known was imprisoned deep inside, waiting for a trigger to reveal itself. For the first time in her life she understood the power and potency of sensuality.

But she had been silent too long, her brows wrinkled in a puzzled frown over stunned blue eyes.

'Alexa?' he said sharply. 'Are you not well?'

His eyes watched the muscles move in the pale length of her throat as she swallowed, then flicked up to a face grown impassive with control. Inwardly she shivered, but she managed to reply in a prim little voice that revealed nothing. 'I'm fine, thank you. I'll go home today.'

'Home?'

The single word was a taunt. All of her antagonism came flooding back. On a snap she said, 'Home, Mr Venetos,' and turned into the room that had once been hers and was now no refuge from something that made her more wary each moment that passed.

She was almost inside when she heard a woman's voice, clear and lazily sensual, from the open window further along. The mistress, she thought dispassionately, the woman Sean admired.

As she showered and brushed her teeth in the small bathroom she couldn't subdue the sheer physical impact that Leon Venetos had on her, from his face with its unusual indications of his dual ancestry in form and colouring, to the easy litheness that had something dangerous in it, a hint of primitive steel and power. She could believe the stories current about him, the man who had inherited millions from his father and set out to turn them into billions. Rumour, based for once on some solid facts, said that he was already there.

And all before he had turned thirty-five!

Alexa knew the workings of the money market intimately, so she had a fair idea of how his wealth had been earned, but she also knew that he liked to amuse himself with other, rather quixotic projects. He had bought a fishing village on one of the Scottish islands so that the villagers could remain there, and another small island in the Pacific had found itself the happy recipient of a small freighter to help shift the copra crop. Obviously he liked islands. It was, she thought sourly, the only nice thing she knew about him.

Her clothes had been unpacked and the suitcase stowed in the bottom of the wardrobe. Rapidly, almost carelessly, she put on a pair of blue slacks and an oversized blue shirt, repacked the case and stripped the bed, remaking it before she left the room, case in hand.

He was waiting in the wide hall at the foot of the stairs, scanning some mail. Alexa came stiffly down, angry with herself for being so acutely conscious of her body. His brows rose.

'Can't you wait to leave us?'

She could have made a smart answer, but contented herself with a pale smile. 'You've been very kind,' she said in her most colourless voice, 'but I want to get the house-cleaning done before it gets too hot.'

He frowned. 'You're in no fit state to do anything like that.'

'It was a migraine, not a brain tumour. I'm fine now.'

He looked as though he wanted to argue with that, but after a level stare from her he shrugged and said smoothly, 'You'll have breakfast before you go.'

Just that. It was not an observation, or a suggestion, it was a straight command, and although she felt edgy and strung up she went docilely with him to a room where the table was set for the meal.

She even managed to eat something, a piece of delicious wholegrain toast, and drink some orange juice, although she blenched when he offered her coffee. Beyond, in the kitchen, she could hear soft movements; the housekeeper, presumably. A large, dark-haired woman, she recalled, who had helped her get into bed the night before. By the time they reached the homestead she had been so sick that she could remember very little of what had happened, but the woman's hands had been gentle and she had made little softly sympathetic noises, like a mother. Raewyn...? Yes, Raewyn Cox.

Leon made polite, formal conversation; her polite, formal responses were interrupted by the sound of a helicopter flying in. Leon frowned, but said smoothly, 'Please excuse me. If you want to read the newspaper while I'm gone, feel free. It's on the sofa by the window.'

But when he had left Alexa didn't look at the newspaper. Instead, her eyes travelled around the room, noting the differences since she had last seen it.

She was in what had originally been a part of the kitchen area; her father had always referred to it as 'the still room'. Now the walls had been replaced by windows, but the floor of worn terracotta tiles was still there, at home with the plants in the internal window-boxes and the comfortable cane furniture. Against one wall was an old French baker's table, its charming cast-iron framework supporting a pale marble top. Wide doors led out on to a terrace and beyond that was the stretch of lawn bordered by pohutukawa trees and the sea.

Very up-market, Alexa thought, as she sipped coffee. Yet whoever had decorated it had been sensible. The room was practical as well as thoroughly in keeping with the rest of the house. She looked pensively at a hova vine that revealed pretty pink-icing flowers beneath the leathery leaves. In winter, even in Northland's notorious rain, this room would be a charming summery refuge.

Nice to have money.

The sound of the helicopter died away into stillness, to be followed by voices. Masculine, and they were not exchanging pleasantries. She heard a light, younger voice say something—she recognised a note of justification. Leon Venetos said something short and succinct, and there was silence. A silence followed by his arrival back in the charming little breakfast-room.

'Are you ready to go?' he asked politely.

Alexa nodded, getting to her feet. 'Yes, of course.'

There was the sound of a step in the passage outside, and a young, brashly masculine voice called, 'Hey, where is everyone?'

Leon did not look particularly pleased. In fact, Alexa thought with pleasure, he looked extremely unamused. A thunderous frown drew his brows together and he strode towards the door with a lean and pantherish stride that boded no good for the newcomer.

However, before he got there the door was flung open and in came a man whose strong resemblance made it clear that they were brothers.

'Chris! I thought I told you to wait for me in the office?'

Not in the least put out by the abrupt and far from friendly question, Chris Venetos smiled at Alexa, only just hiding the momentary astonishment that had shown in his face when he saw her. 'I wanted to ask you something,' he said cheerfully. 'Aren't you going to introduce us, Leon?'

His brother looked a little taken aback, and Chris laughed and came into the room, his bold dark eyes openly appreciative as they surveyed Alexa. 'Hi, I'm Chris Venetos.'

Smiling, she held out her hand, but before she could give her name Leon said curtly. 'This is Alexa Severn. She was ill last night and is on her way back to Honeymoon Bay now.'

There was instant recognition in the dark eyes, followed by a cynical reappraisal that brought Alexa's head up. With the suave grace he shared with his brother, Chris took her hand and kissed it.

'How fortunate for us all that we are here to give succour to the wounded,' he murmured.

Alexa removed her hand and gave him a weary, rather sardonic smile. 'Isn't it just,' she said deliberately, revising her first favourable opinion of him. Clearly the Venetos clan all suffered from cynicism and a grossly inflated opinion of their own importance.

Fairness prompted her to concede that perhaps they had a right to be wary. From the snippets of gossip her mother insisted on regaling her with, she knew that men like these, with all the money and power they controlled, didn't need to be pleasant or good-looking to be attractive to many women. It was no wonder they developed a siege mentality. However, her feelings had been rubbed raw by Leon's barely concealed contempt. She was damned if she was going to put up with anything from a boy who looked to be no more than twenty.

He looked taken aback when her cool scorn registered, revealing his youth in a moment of uncertainty with a quick flush along the cheekbones that would become as stark as his brother's in a few years. He sent Leon a swift, self-conscious glance which was met by a steely regard.

'I think,' Leon said deliberately, 'you had better come with me. I'll get you the information you want.'

His brother smiled apprehensively, gave a slight shrug and threw Alexa a comical glance of entreaty that made a mockery of the cynicism he had affected earlier. When they had left the room she wondered whether perhaps Chris had been imitating the brother he so clearly was more than a little in awe of.

Leon had to be at least thirteen years older, and he possessed a cold air of authority that any younger brother would have found intimidating. She wondered what it would be like to have brothers or sisters, and reminded herself with an odd little shock that she had a couple. Half-siblings, of course. Her father's second wife had presented him with two small sons. Unfortunately her jealousy made it unpleasant for Alexa to see much of her father, so that beyond their names and ages she knew very little of her half-brothers.

Her shoulders lifted in the slightest of shrugs. She had never known what it was like to be a member of a happy family, and it was too late to mourn it now. Thrusting the lurking self-pity into the back of her mind, she went into the kitchen to thank the housekeeper for looking after her, assuring her that she felt well enough to climb mountains this morning.

'Do you often get those migraines?' the woman asked.

'Not often. I think they're mostly tension. Jet lag wouldn't have helped, either.'

The housekeeper smiled, clearly curious and clearly determined not to give in to it. 'Well, if you need any help, you ring.'

Cynically wondering just what Leon Venetos would say to the woman's kind offer, Alexa thanked her and took her leave, waiting at the door beside her suitcase. A Range Rover waited on the driveway of crushed shell—that at least hadn't changed—and the oleander bushes that held their silky flowers against the stiff dark leaves had been there for generations. But even from here she could see that money had been poured into the rest of the station. There were new buildings, older ones repaired and repainted, and one of the workers' cottages had been replaced by a bigger house.

Leon Venetos came up behind her with noiseless footsteps as she was bending to pet a small kitten that had come wandering up.

'He has your colouring,' he observed, watching her through half-closed eyes. 'Hair black as soot and eyes that win a contest with the summer sky.'

Alexa despised herself for blushing, especially when she saw the ironic lift to the corners of his mouth, but she said calmly, 'He's a sweet thing.'

'Raewyn Cox's. The housekeeper's.' As though irritated with himself, he said, 'Right, are you ready to go?'

'Yes.' Had been for some time, in fact, so why was he hustling her out as though she had suddenly begun to contaminate his pretty house? Perhaps the mistress was on her way down, and he didn't want them to meet.

'I'll take you back in the Range Rover. Hop in.'

She didn't protest. His tone made it quite obvious that he was not going to be put off. No doubt, she thought with savage amusement, he wanted to make quite sure that she was seen off the property!

But it was hard to remain offended when she was only too eager to go back and they were driving through a day of gold and blue and green, fresh and sweet as only early summer could be.

The impulse that had brought her back to the island had been the right one. She needed solitude, and the timeless truths of land and sea and sky to rebuild her life again. Yes, she had chosen her refuge well. If only it did not contain Leon Venetos!

Half-way up the hill that separated the two bays he said casually, 'How stupid of Sam Darcy to try to kill himself because you left him.'

The shock of the attack rendered her silent for a few seconds, but she countered stiffly, 'I don't have to listen to that sort of——'

'Oh, come now, Alexa, I can't imagine that you haven't heard worse! Women—and men—who prostitute themselves for whatever reason have to learn to live with contempt. If you didn't know where you were headed, you must have been remarkably unsophisticated! I can understand why he lost his head over you—you are remarkably beautiful—but it astounds me that he didn't see that women like you are easily bought for the price of a few jewels. To put you into his firm and then promote you above men who had been there for years—no doubt it pleased his ego and yours, but it was a recipe for disaster. Better to——'

Sheer savage rage brought a bite to her tone as she interrupted. 'I was good at my job, Mr Venetos. Nobody ever questioned my skill.'

'Not to your face, perhaps. It was well known in the city that you were out of your depth.'

The amused scorn in his voice made anger sing in her brain but she reined it in, subdued it. When she spoke her voice was remote and cool, emptied of all emotion.

'I can't see any point in prolonging this—tirade. You needn't worry about seeing any more of me.'

He paused, long enough to set her nerves screaming, then said sardonically, 'A consummation devoutly to be wished,' and brought the Range Rover to a halt outside the appalling fence he had ordered around her land, leaving her shaking and furious, whipping up her rage to hide the intense desolation beneath it.

It was all a lie, of course. She had been very good at her job, with an intuitive and rapid understanding of the market which came, perhaps, from the fact that she was a brilliant mathematician. She had been toppled because Sam had made the mistake of becoming too fond of his protégée, and the even graver mistake of admitting to his wife how he felt.

Alexa winced, remembering her dismay when she realised that her mentor, the man she admired and respected as a friend, had fallen in love with her. She had desperately tried to avoid the issue, praying that he would recover quickly when he realised that she had no such feelings for him. Instead he had asked her, gently yet inexorably, whether there was any hope for him, and when she had said no, he had said that he would try to make her change her mind. He had meant it, too.

Worried and frightened, she had wondered how she was going to deal with the situation, but the initiative had been seized from both of them. Somehow his wife had found out.

It had been a nightmare. Alexa could understand why the executives in the bank had leapt on to the bandwagon and disowned her. They had found it almost impossible to deal with the fact that a woman, much younger than they and without their years of striving and experience, had raced ahead of them. All the time that she had worked there she had been made aware of their resentment. She had not been surprised at their attitude, but she had been confident of eventually winning them over. Without boasting, she knew she had been more than competent.

She could not understand Sam's wife, who had behaved in what seemed to Alexa to be a totally bizarre fashion. Mrs Darcy had hated her because she believed Alexa had taken her son's rightful place. Not a particularly intelligent woman, Sam's wife had refused to accept that their son was simply not equipped to follow his father. Alexa could—just—sympathise with the fierce maternal feelings that had driven Mrs Darcy to her disastrous course of wailing about her husband's infatuation to a famous gossip columnist. But the stupidity of the woman's subsequent involvement with the Press made her cringe whenever she thought about it—which was almost all the time.

Once the gossip columnist had printed his juicy bit of news, everyone implicated had been inundated with journalists, eager for blood and copy. Alexa had refused to speak to anyone; Sam had issued a dignified rebuttal of everything his wife had said, but Mrs Darcy had gone on to bigger and more sensational things, charging that her husband was obsessed to the point of madness with Alexa, that he had told her that he would do whatever was necessary to marry her, that he would allow nothing to stand in his way...

She hadn't cared for her husband's pain, or the standing of the business. Wilfully, defiantly, she had tarnished the name of everyone concerned when she accused Alexa of seducing Sam, and been openly triumphant when the subsequent firestorm of publicity had persuaded an appalled Alexa to resign and run for home.

But none of that was any concern of the man who took her suitcase from the big vehicle and carried it across the lawn to dump it on to the terrace. What was it to him? If he had any dealings with the bank at all he must know that the rumours about her professional incompetence were lies, and what other reasons could he have for being so contemptuous?

'Thank you.' Her voice was frosty.

He smiled mockingly. 'I'd have done the same for anyone. Tell me, have you any diesel for the generator?'

Feeling a complete fool, she said, 'I don't know. I haven't been to the shed. I just assumed that there'd be some.'

'We'll check it out. If you haven't got any I can lend you a drum.'

There wasn't. Alexa bit her lip, angry with herself for neglecting to arrange it. She thought dismally that he had every right to doubt her competence at anything!

'It's just as well I thought to bring a drum, isn't it?' he said sarcastically.

He had the equipment and the strength to get the drum up into the shed, and once there made her turn the generator on so that he could give her a quick lesson in the care and maintenance of the beast, before at last he went, leaving her exhausted and oddly bereft.

She waited until the sound of the engine had died away completely then went out on to the beach, and stood in the brilliant heat and looked around her.

It was just a beach, like thousands of other beaches, yet for her it had become a symbol of a happiness she had thought she might never attain again, an innocence lost beyond recovery. Golden-tawny sand, hard and damp beneath her feet, powdery and hot as Hades above the high-tide mark. Low headlands of red-ochre rock beneath garlands of trees, and the naked gold muscles of the hills all around, swelling smoothly to the summit of the island. To one side of the bay a tiny stream ran out through the tall cabbage trees and spiky clumps of flax. Her eyes followed the bright greenery that marked its path up the valley until it disappeared behind the flank of the hill. Beyond was the spring, dammed to pump out a constant supply of water to the small corrugated iron tank on its stand behind the house.

Low, built of wood that had faded to a silver-grey, sheltered by pergolas still greened by creepers, the cottage had been renovated by her mother when she was still trying to make a life for herself on the island. Guests had used it, some paying, most friends, or friends of friends.

Alexa remembered some of the people who had stayed here. Many were honeymooners, continuing a tradition that had given the bay its name. But most of all she remembered the febrile excitement with which her mother had greeted them, the eagerness with which she had suggested they finish their holidays with a few days spent at the homestead.

Well, she was happy enough now, even though all her plans for her daughter had been shattered in the furnace of scandal and notoriety. Her second marriage to a barrister had satisfied those longings that had driven her away from the island. If she ever thought of the years she had spent trying to fall out of love with her first husband, she never admitted it.

But for a while, to amuse herself, she had poured all her creative ingenuity into redesigning the little house, turning it from a nondescript little bach, as holiday homes were called in northern New Zealand, to a small but sophisticated house that wouldn't have been out of place in Acapulco or the Riviera.

Floors of ceramic tile were easy to keep clear of the ubiquitous sand, the walls painted in cool, pale summery colours were still in excellent condition, and although the windows were encrusted with the salt of too many winter storms, they were intact. Alexa stood for a long moment, her blue eyes smoky with dreams and memories, then walked up across the sand and into the house.

The first thing to do was to open the windows. She turned into the bedroom and did the same there, pausing for a moment to check the wide double bed. Surprisingly, and fortunately, the mattress smelt fine, not damp as it could have been after all these years. But, just in case, she dragged it off the base and struggled with it across the room and out through the wide glass doors on to the terrace, propping it up in the sun against the wall of the house.

Then she went into the kitchen and tested the taps. Yes, water came out, although it smelt a bit stale. And the hot taps even gave hot water, due to the solar panels in the roof. The small kitchen was neat but showing the effects of years of disuse.

Looking around with a frown of distaste, she decided to wash down the floors and all the surfaces in the kitchen. For a moment she stood looking out of the wide doors across the terrace and over the sea; the temptation to see if the hammock was still in the store-room was almost irresistible, but Alexa was not one to put off unpleasant things, and with a wistful sigh she rooted beneath the sink for some detergent.

Hours later, as the sun was sinking and the air turning that exquisite purple that is summer, she straightened up, a hand going automatically to the small of her back to massage the muscles there. She was most emphatically not accustomed to manual work!

She lifted the heavy black mass of her hair up from her sticky nape, feeling grubby and worn out, as well as hungry. It didn't occur to her that this was the first time she had been hungry for months; since the storm had burst, in fact. But her efforts had been worth it. The kitchen and the sitting-room were clean and sweet-smelling, and the bedroom was ready for her.

Groaning a little, she turned to make herself a sandwich of the wholegrain bread she liked so much. When the couple of loaves she had brought with her had been eaten she would have to rely on crispbreads.

How was Sam? Still fighting for his life? Or dead?

All day she had pushed the thought to the back of her mind. Now, forced to contemplate it, she found the tears coming. Before long she was sitting on the bed in the dark, weeping as though her heart would break.

She had dismissed Sam's protestations of love, convinced that he was suffering from a mid-life crisis fuelled by the fact that he and his wife were at loggerheads over his refusal to give his son a position of power. She had resigned because she was sure that, once she was gone, he would return to his wife, but this latest development seemed to indicate that perhaps Mrs Darcy had been correct when she stated that he was obsessed with Alexa. Poor Sam.

It was, she thought angrily, so *unnecessary*. Before all this blew up she had been happy. Oh, there had always been the feeling that by going into commerce she had betrayed what she knew to be a rare talent for pure mathematics. Her professor at the university had been horrified, but her mother had persuaded her, and been so proud of her...

However, she hadn't believed her when Alexa had tried to convince her that she had not sold herself to Sam.

'Then why has his wife left him?' she demanded, angry because her friends were all whispering about her suddenly notorious daughter. Her long, slim finger stabbed distastefully at the headlines in a newspaper that normally she would not have had in the house. 'And how is it that you have gone so far, so fast? It hints in here that you were hopeless at your job.'

'And do you believe that?'

Her mother flushed, seeming to realise what she had been implying. In a more moderate tone she had said, 'I must say that I have wondered. I know how good you are at figures, Alexa, but it did seem strange that with no experience at all you should rise so far and so fast.'

'I see.'

Alexa's quiet reply brought forth a display of anger that revealed how upset her mother was. 'And you haven't denied it!'

'Do you think anyone would believe me if I did?' She didn't say that the thought of talking to the Press made her feel ill.

'You could at least try! I'm a modern woman, Alexa, but how could you have been so indiscreet? For his wife to find out! It says here that Samuel Darcy has never been known for his love affairs, but he's in his forties, and everyone knows how men get then.'

'A mid-life crisis?' Alexa's beautiful mouth pulled into a travesty of a smile. It seemed odd to hear her own convictions on her mother's lips.

'Well, if he wasn't having one before, he certainly is now! His wife has left him, his own board is turning on him to try to get rid of him, and what do you do? Nothing!'

Alexa was very tired. She had come to her mother for some sort of support, but it hadn't surprised her too much to be greeted with this. Wearily, she said, 'What do you suggest I do? If I deny it, no one will believe me. If I resign, it will be taken as a sign that the bloodhounds are right.'

'And if you don't resign,' her mother said crisply, 'you'll be sacked. You and Darcy both. As for being right—well, I don't know of anybody who believes you are innocent. I am sick of fielding impertinent questions from everyone I meet!'

So for Sam's sake and her mother's she had resigned, and without seeing him had fled back to sanctuary in New Zealand, much to everyone's relief.

But Sam had tried to commit suicide. Had she so gravely misjudged his feelings? Or was it that this middle-aged passion was very much stronger than the affection and propinquity she had assumed it to be?

At the start of their association he had been fatherly. He had been so proud of her success that she had sometimes wondered a little uneasily if she had taken his son's place in his affections. And she had worked her heart out, both for him, because he had had faith in her, and for her own satisfaction.

But in the last few months the easy affection and pride had turned to something she had not recognised. Not at first, anyway, until she had been forced to confront it. He had begun to treat her less as a colleague and friend, more as a woman he wanted to court.

Where she had made the mistake, of course, was in ignoring the signs, hoping her inchoate fears were wrong. Perhaps if she had been more experienced when it came to men she would have been able to deal better with the situation, tactfully scotching any hopes he might have early on, so that they would have been able to return to their old standing.

But she hadn't known how to go about it, and while she was dithering he had spoken, and his wife had found out.

At last the tears stopped. Surprisingly enough she drifted off to sleep without too much difficulty, and woke to the kind of radiant, tender morning that she had forgotten. The sky was glowing, the light breeze fresh and sweet-smelling; even the quarrelsome gulls seemed to have forgotten their never-ending battle for food and precedence and only gave vent to a mild purring call. The sun danced on the dancing waves. Just over the horizon a freighter made its way down the coast towards Auckland. It looked as though there were two strange vessels there keeping perfect distance apart.

Alexa picked a golden babaco off the tree to eat with her coffee and toast. In spite of everything, in spite of her disillusion and her sick worry about Sam, her spirits rose with the sun. She had forgotten how lovely it could be here. Or perhaps, after the trauma of her parents' separation and her exile, she had repressed the memories because they only caused her pain.

Until then, she hadn't realised just how much tension she had been suffering from. Migraines had been one symptom; now that she was home, and always providing Leon Venetos stayed away, they might no longer plague her. She had never had one until her name began appearing in the headlines.

After breakfast she continued cleaning the house, working easily and hard, until just before lunch she looked out to see a flotilla of yachts come by, sails set and buoyant in the light breeze. As she watched, the leading one went about just outside the bay; a moment later, the sails began to fold and an anchor rattled down. It couldn't have been premeditated, because as a dinghy headed ashore the others sailed on past, then came about and tacked back.

Alexa resisted her first involuntary retreat. She did not want visitors, but it was paranoid to expect all who came near to be journalists. Nevertheless, she waited warily on the terrace, her face shuttered.

There were two people in the dinghy, a man and a woman; they dragged the small craft up the beach and advanced, looking a little self-conscious under her gaze. As they came closer she relaxed. They were tall and lithe and deeply tanned, with an indefinable aura which proclaimed that they were Americans.

Sure enough, it was in a pleasantly nasal accent that the man greeted her. 'Hi, my name's Jarrod Kyle, and this is my wife Heather.'

A little stiffly Alexa said her name, watching closely as they shook hands with her. Neither of them showed any reaction, and she relaxed a little more.

'We've just arrived in New Zealand and, although it's full of pretty spots, this must be one of the most beautiful we've seen,' the woman said, surveying the beach with real appreciation.

Alexa smiled. 'I love it.'

Jarrod gave her a warm smile. 'I guess you do! Are you the owner of this land? I'll tell you why I'd like to know. We're part of that little flotilla out there; all of us have come down from the Islands to escape the hurricane season, and although we just loved the Bay of Islands we found it awfully full of people this time of year! We're looking for a quieter place to spend Christmas Day, somewhere the kids can run about and enjoy themselves.'

Alexa wanted to refuse. She had planned to treat the next day as though it was another ordinary summer day, and the thought of children with their innocent, greedy enjoyment hurt. But even as she went to say no, she saw the infinitesimal tightening of muscle in the couple that meant they were bracing themselves for rejection.

So instead of a polite refusal she said, 'What would you want to do?'

'Well, we'd just anchor in one of the bays and have a barbecue and a little party, let the kids run around a bit, play a few games.' He smiled and went on carefully, 'We'd watch them to make sure they didn't stray, and we don't go in for orgies, or anything like that.'

She believed him. Smiling, she found herself saying, 'I own only this bay, so you'd have to anchor in here.'

Quick disappointment was hastily hidden. 'Oh well, you wouldn't want——'

Hastily, before she could change her mind, she said, 'No, that would be all right. I don't mind. It would be rather nice to have children here for Christmas. Only I'm afraid they'd be confined to this bay and the area inside the fence. I'm not on the best of terms with the owner of the rest of the island and he's threatened me with trespass. He owns riparian rights, so that means the other beaches are out of bounds.'

They didn't look surprised. Perhaps in America landowners did that sort of thing all the time. Or was it that everyone, even summer sailors, knew that the Venetos Corporation didn't want visitors on the island?

Within an hour all five yachts were anchored in the bay. Alexa counted a Canadian flag, as well as one from Germany and the Union Jack, and even the vertical green white and red stripes of Italy. A truly multinational fleet, she mused, and envied them their freedom, their peaceful way of life, even the natural dangers that they faced. At least a storm at sea was impersonal!

By evening she had accepted an invitation to join them in their Christmas festivities, and spent a very cheerful hour pointing out to the six children where to collect driftwood and fallen branches to keep the barbecue supplied. They were delightful, from the fat toddler who spoke only Italian to a very adult ten-year-old who slipped from English to French to German without any difficulty, frequently tossing in words from various Pacific Islands, most of which Alexa recognised from their resemblance to similar words in the Maori language.

Eventually an enormous pile of bleached wood reposed on one side of the beach, well above high-water mark, and the children made their way to their respective floating homes. Alexa was startled to see that it was after five. Normally she would have gone for a swim, but she had no bathing suit and the presence of the yachts prevented her from swimming in her underwear. A little sadly she went into the now shining house.

When she had left London she had packed summer clothes, and not too many of them, but she found now a length of cotton she had bought on a trip to Indonesia. Tied in a variety of ways it could double as dress or wrap, and the batik pattern in pale terracotta and blue suited her very well. She had never worn it in England; the exotic pattern looked out of place there. Here, however, it came into its own. It could cover up her underclothes and become a pleasantly informal swimsuit. She opened the drawer and fished it out.

Sam had been with her when she had bought it. She was wondering bleakly how he was when a voice called her name.

Instantly her head came up. How dared Leon Venetos come back? Rigidly erect, she marched through the door and on to the terrace, the length of material still clutched in her hands.

He was standing surveying the fleet of yachts, his dark brows drawn together in a frown that pleased her immensely, and for a moment she had the luxury of being able to watch him unobserved. Another funny little clutch of sensation in the pit of her stomach startled her as her eyes wandered from the gleaming sandy gold of his hair, down the arrogantly sculpted profile, even further down to stop finally on the lean, strongly muscled length of his thighs. He was, she admitted reluctantly, a splendid male animal. It was no wonder she felt a tingle of shameful attraction.

After all, she was a woman. And with no experience, so he also possessed the lure of the unknown, the forbidden.

He turned his head and her lashes fell to hide her open scrutiny. Maddeningly, the instinctive retreat must have made her look like a submissive idiot.

The strong cruel mouth curved into a cynical little smile. 'I think you're good to look at too,' he said softly. 'Do you need a man, Alexa?'

Colour scorched along her cheekbones. 'Don't be disgusting!'

'Didn't you realise that using your delectable body as a bargaining counter in your career was going to lay you open to disgusting remarks like that?' He wasn't in the least upset by her shock. The dark eyes gleamed with worldly amusement as he openly and disrespectfully looked her over, his gaze lingering longest on her mouth and hips and the curves of her breasts. Incredibly, her skin prickled as though it had been smoothed with velvet, or touched with a feather.

She was speechless, only the outrage in her expression conveying her emotions. Not in the least intimidated he finished coolly, 'After all, if you put yourself on the block you must expect the prospective buyer to check out the goods.'

'You are not a prospective buyer!'

She could have kicked herself for the inanity of her reply but sheer fury had numbed her normally swift brain.

And he took advantage of it, that sinister smile touching his mouth. 'I could be,' he said calmly.

She had thought that nothing could ever be said to her that would shock her again. However, his cool effrontery staggered her more than all the lascivious hints and innuendoes of the Press. She closed her eyes, and turned her head away while anger, steel-hard and vicious, came to her aid.

'What did you say?'

If she had had some faint hope of shaming him into backing down, she was soon disillusioned. He said blandly, 'I could be a market for those wares you sell so dearly. I find you very attractive, and I'm reasonably sure that you want me.'

'If I didn't,' she said, sweetly vicious, 'no doubt any deal would be off.'

He laughed. 'Not necessarily. However, I was doing you the honour of assuming that you are not a prostitute and that you sleep only with men you want. Or men who will help you attain whatever ends you have in mind. Am I right?'

Her lashes dropped, echoing the corners of her mouth. She was so angry that she couldn't think. After a taut few seconds she said steadily, 'My ethical standards are not going to make any difference, as I am certainly not ever going to sleep with you.'

'Now that,' he mused in a tone that sent a sudden *frisson* through her body, 'that is almost a challenge. I find it hard to resist challenges.'

The taste of danger was bitter on her tongue. Her lashes flew up and, dry-mouthed, she watched him come towards her, moving with a lithe predatory grace that shouldn't have belonged to such a big man.

'No,' she whispered, but it was too late.

His hands were quite gentle on her shoulders, but she couldn't move because something was happening inside her that robbed her limbs of strength. It almost seemed as though he had the power to render her paralysed, both will and body.

He was smiling, a cruel little smile that made him a threat, and before she could respond physically to it his mouth touched hers.

She had been kissed before. Most of them she had enjoyed, yet she had never known what desire was. Nothing in her life before had ever touched this peak. His mouth was magic, torment; it drove her beyond the realms of normality and into a place where the centre dissolved and she was left whirling helplessly in a torrent of sensuality, drained of all powers of resistance.

Terrified, bewildered, her body singing with sensation, she surrendered beneath the seeking incitement.

CHAPTER THREE

ALEXA could not tell him that it had never happened before, because that would give him some sort of power over her. Numbly, she said, 'I want you to go. Now.'

But before she had time to retreat behind the mask he put his hand under her chin and tilted her face up to an unsparing appraisal. His hard scrutiny searched out the trembling passionate softness of her lips, the astonishment clouding her eyes, and he laughed beneath his breath. 'You look surprised. I wonder... Have you always been completely in control before, Alexa, doling out sex the way a mother hands out sweets, reinforcing the behaviour you want to encourage but essentially untouched by it?'

Lashes drooping, she turned her head away, anything to escape that knowing gaze, but she carried with her the memory of his eyes, harsh yet still oddly bright, and she knew, with an instinct that had just that moment flowered, that he was using insults to distance himself from what had happened because he, too, had been thrown off balance.

It was an enslavement of the senses, for him as well as her.

Beneath the screen of her lashes her brain was recovering from the fumes of sensual longing. She would not admit to anything—surely he wouldn't be interested in a woman he had stigmatised as little better than a prostitute? He had been punishing her for some reason. Alexa understood some things about men; she had had to deal with them in her years at university and at work, and she knew that it was difficult for most of them to accept that a woman could be good at anything they considered to be a traditional masculine pursuit. Like working the international money market.

So she was not particularly surprised that he should feel the need to put her down, even though he seemed very confident—too arrogant in his masculine self-assurance to need it boosted with out-of-date assumptions.

She stepped away, wondering poignantly if he saw women only as important for bed and child-rearing.

'No answer?' he mocked, and tucked his shirt into his shorts, smiling sardonically as the ready colour flowed into her skin again. 'Perhaps you're wise. After all, what can you say? That you melt in my arms like honey, that when I touch you——'

'Possibly I find it expedient to do so,' she snapped.

His laughter was mocking and mirthless. 'Oh, I imagine you do. However, I know that you weren't thinking of expediency when you kissed me, because I felt exactly the same.'

'You are conceited.' Her voice was uninflected, smooth and bored.

He grinned. 'Possibly. But I'm not stupid, and I know more than I care to about your sex. Admit it, Alexa, you want me. I don't know why you should be so antagonistic, as I've made it clear that the feeling is mutual.'

'The casual desire of any man for any woman?' She didn't have to feign the scorn in her tones. 'Sorry, I'm not interested.'

He looked at her, long and lethally, the cold insolence in his eyes hurting her deep in her soul. 'I see,' he said, after a tense moment. 'So you really have a commercial attitude to your beautiful body. Strictly *quid pro quo*. Well, I'm not playing that game, Alexa. I've never had to pay for sex before, and I'm not starting now.'

She should have been triumphant, so it was strange that her heart felt as though someone had carved a chunk out of it. He turned to go and she knew that she wasn't going to see him again. As he stepped down on to the long grass at the base of the terrace he said curtly. 'See that nobody from those yachts sets foot on my property.'

Alexa's hand stole to her tender mouth. She held her breath until he had gone, and then she began to shake, her face as white as paper. He had done what no man had ever done before; he had terrified her. And her swift, incandescent response to his kisses had devastated her.

Aloud she said, 'I must be a masochist.'

Fortunately she had no time to brood. Two of the children came running up the beach to tell her that they had decided to sing carols on the beach that night, and would she like to come? It provided the perfect escape from the turbulence of her self-recriminations.

She washed some clothes out and hung them on the line before making herself a small meal with some of the vegetables she had brought across from the mainland. Her appetite had not come back, and if she had to see any more of Leon Venetos, she thought grimly, it never would.

Around seven o'clock, when the sun was losing its heat and the little breeze had died completely, the dinghies came ashore with their cargoes of excited children. They begged to be allowed a bonfire, so they lit a small one and sat around on sand still warm from the sun. One of the fathers had a guitar and for a while they drank red wine from a cask and sang a medley of songs; nursery rhymes from various countries, songs like *'Frère Jacques'* that were truly international.

One of the children demanded, 'Sing us a New Zealand song, Alexa.'

She laughed and asked if she could borrow the guitar. Her voice was pleasant and she had no difficulty with *'Po karekare ana'*, the sweetly haunting melody lingering across the quiet waters of the bay.

'Teach us it. Please.'

She smiled down into the rapt face of the small boy at her feet, and taught them the words, following that with a stick game that ended up as a riotous round, with everyone bellowing out in turn, until at last it dissolved into laughter and chaos. Alexa went to hand the guitar back to its owner, but he said, 'No, no, you play much better—so if you do not mind...?'

She began to pick out chords, her fingers sliding delicately across the strings, and the sun dipped below the horizon in a glory of gold and salmon pink that faded into blue, the flakes of cloud turning into scales of mother-of-pearl. Someone began to sing a carol and, as the dusk came down about them and the waves hushed crisply on to the sand, they sang all of the old Christmas songs, remembering nostalgically those they had left behind. They spoke of their various traditions, and laughed, and if some voices were a bit shaky, well, everyone pretended not to notice.

The moon rose, huge and round in a coppery nest of clouds, then sprang free and chased the stars away. The smaller children were asleep, the bigger ones yawning. In one of the sudden hushes that occur when everyone knows it's time to make the first move to go, but no one wants to, Alexa began to sing 'Silent Night' unaccompanied, her eyes fixed on the dying embers. Clear and sweet, the first verse echoed out across the moonpath; then they joined in, all in their own language.

Afterwards there was silence, broken only by the whimper of a sleeping child. As if afraid to break the spell, they slipped away, leaving Alexa to throw a bucket of sea-water over the flames. She was almost back at the house when her eyes caught movement up on the hill beneath a tall cabbage tree. She tried to tell herself that it was a cow—a bird, but she saw the moon catch a head of silver, and knew that Leon Venetos had been watching them.

No doubt to make sure they didn't trespass on his beloved land, she thought, and on a sudden sour impulse waved.

To her astonishment there was an answering wave, then he turned and strode away across the hill and down into Homestead Bay.

Christmas Day was, for once, fine and sunny. Alexa had been dreading it, but apart from a few nostalgic moments when she went to bed it was unalloyed pleasure from start to finish. The sweets she had made the day before were greeted with joy by the children, and the salads with acclamation by the adults. They roasted lamb on a spit over the coals of the bonfire, swam and played games, and finally ate beneath the low branches of an enormous pohutukawa tree, laughing when the faint warm breeze blew the scarlet needles down into the salads.

Afterwards everyone slept it off, and there were more games and a story-telling session, until at last they went back and she went to bed. This time there was no unseen watcher up on the hill.

They left the next morning. Before they went they insisted on handing over some stores, and one couple, the

Americans, took a list and promised to drop off groceries when they sailed past the next day.

Alexa accepted and waved them goodbye with gratitude and anger. Gratitude because they were so kind, and anger because if Leon Venetos weren't so bloody-minded she wouldn't have to rely on other people's generosity and kindness. Just for a moment, as they were almost ready to leave, she found herself wondering if perhaps she should go with them and find some other place to hide in and lick her wounds.

Then she thought of the insults he had paid her, and her face stiffened. I'll be damned if I let him run me off the place, she thought bleakly.

She swam after they left, at first in the sarong. The sea was as smooth and silky and warm as any tropical ocean she had ever experienced; after a few minutes she stood up and pulled the clinging fabric of the sarong free of her body and threw it up on to the sand before revelling in the feel of the water across her body. She would have liked to sunbathe naked, but the hills around the bay made good vantage points and she couldn't forget that Leon Venetos had watched from up there the night before Christmas.

After the swim she showered, frowning when she had to turn the tap full on to get enough pressure. She could well have used most of the water in the tank, but it should have refilled from the spring.

She took the broom outside and tested the tank. A few sharp taps up from the bottom revealed that, far from refilling, it was almost empty. Just to make sure she tapped it again, her mouth tightening with dismay as the hollow ringing sound that denoted emptiness contrasted sharply with the noise from the bottom. A little judicious tapping up the side of the tank revealed that she had about a foot of water left. Not enough for a day, not even if she was careful.

Clearly something had gone wrong with either the supply from the spring or the pump up there. Unfortunately, to check it she was going to have to cross Leon Venetos's land. And although she was not afraid of him, she thought it might be a good idea to wait until the moon was up and everyone was safely inside their houses before going to check on the wretched thing.

She had little appetite for dinner, and not even her mirror's strictures on her pallor and loss of weight could make her force down the half avocado she thought she might eat. Deciding that she would have it when she got back from her mission, she contented herself with a long glass of soda water.

For some reason she had a sickish feeling in her stomach, and when at last the quiet evening had faded into the splendour of the night her self-mockery didn't prevent her from dressing in dark jeans and a black sleeveless T-shirt. And before swinging over the fence she looked long and carefully around, her eyes searching the hills.

Of course there was nothing there beyond large cattle, heads down as they grazed. She gave a swift, derisory smile, muttered a few words in which 'James Bond' figured, and walked lithely over the crisp grass to the cleft in the hills that hid the spring.

Head bent, she followed the path of the underground pipeline as she searched for a tell-tale lush patch of grass that would reveal a leak in it. Nothing showed.

She frowned. Perhaps the hose intake was below the level of the water. But that had never happened before. The spring had never dried up in the worst of droughts.

Puffing slightly, she walked around the side of the hill and down through scratchy sweet-smelling *manuka* and tall tree-ferns, ghostly in the moonlight. The spring had always been fenced off, so the undergrowth was thick and lush; she had to push her way through it, and once she swore softly under her breath as a twig sprang across her face, scratching it slightly.

It was not much easier going with the torch switched on, but at least she could avoid some of the obstacles. Muttering softly, she climbed past the sword-like leaves of great clumps of flax, her nostrils quivering at the fresh dank scent of water. Yes, the spring was still running; even before she got to the pool she could hear the soft chirrup of the tiny stream as it ran down over the rocks towards the sea.

The spring was pumping out its bounty from the depths of the earth, but someone had pulled the pipe out of the water and thrown it up on to the bank, and the small shed that housed the pump had had a padlock put on to the door so that no one could get in.

If Leon Venetos had been there at that moment Alexa would have killed him.

His pettiness made her normally equable temper boil over into such fury that she actually ground her teeth before reason asserted itself, and the pounding in her head eased into a dull ache. She sat down on a patch of dry ground and looked more carefully around.

It was easy enough to see why it had been done. On the opposite side of the small pool another black polythene pipe reached down into the water; she thought of the cattle troughs on the newly subdivided paddocks, and the tiny native trees on the sere flanks of the hills, and understood. But there was enough water to keep them all supplied. And the fact that the cottage had not been used for some years was no excuse for this piece of spite.

To her intense astonishment—and chagrin—Alexa found herself wondering whether Leon knew about this. Perhaps his manager had taken it into his own hands to do it?

Instantly repressing what was clearly a suicidal impulse to fool herself, she got to her feet. Of course Leon had given the order to do this. It was, she thought viciously, just the sort of thing he would do. However, he was not going to get away with it. She thought hard for a few moments and finally took an earring from her ear, straightening out the hook. With half-closed eyes she moved the thin wire around inside the keyhole in the padlock. After a tense few moments she felt the mechanism ease into place and the lock sprang open.

Thank heavens for the sense of curiosity which had persuaded her to discover from her best friend's husband how to pick locks, she thought with a wry smile. Thank you, Jake, who, when not writing plays which made some critics suggest cautiously that perhaps he was the greatest English playwright of the twentieth century, enjoyed himself immensely by producing brilliant and equally skilfully crafted thrillers.

One wet afternoon he had shown her and Cathy how to pick a lock, as well as five easy ways to break into a car and a highly illegal method of making untraceable telephone calls. It was just as well they were all very moral people, she thought with a snort of repressed laughter.

She pushed the end of the hose into the water, then went back to survey the dark interior of the little hut. Fortunately she wasn't afraid of spiders, as the interior was liberally festooned with webs. Her hand hovered above a switch. It was off, and presumably to get water from here to the tank it needed to be on. Grimacing, and hoping that she wasn't about to blow the thing up, she switched it on.

It purred into life as smoothly as though it had never been padlocked away. A little weakly she sat down and waited, afraid to leave it in case something drastic happened. However, it chugged softly on while the level of the water in the rocky little pool sank slowly as the greedy pipe dragged the water out.

After what seemed an age but was probably no more than twenty minutes or so, Alexa judged that the tanks at the bach would be full enough to keep her going for a few days. She turned the switch off and put the padlock back, pushing the hasp into place with a malicious grin. Then she hauled the pipe out of the water and arranged it carefully, as close as she could remember, back where it had lain before. Still grinning, she made her way back through the undergrowth, arriving a few minutes later at the fence that marked the edge of the little gulley.

Just in case, she switched off the torch and walked out from the *tea-trees* into the moonlight.

A dark form rose from the slope of the hill and Leon Venetos said silkily, 'Trespassing, Alexa? I warned you about that, if you remember.'

She gave a little sigh and, for the first time in her life, fainted.

When she woke it was to find herself stretched out on the ground with someone pouring gallons of cold water over her face. At her choked gasp the ruthless first aid stopped.

Weakly, her heart still thundering in her chest and her head whirling in a most disconcerting manner, she spluttered, 'Where am—oh, no!'

'Oh, yes.' His voice was not quite as smooth as normal. She was glad that something had the power to shake his massive self-assurance. 'Do you think you could sit up now?'

He slipped his arm around her shoulders and helped, ignoring the stiffness his touch produced. Alexa's head gave a final spin then settled more or less steadily back into place. She tried to ease away from his hold, but he kept his arm very firmly across her shoulder and said meditatively, 'Somehow I don't think you are geared for a life of crime. Or do you make a habit of fainting at moments of stress?'

Waspishly she demanded, 'Why are you so sure I fainted? Perhaps I decided to do it to put you at a disadvantage.'

'Oh, no.' He sounded so positive that she twisted her head to look up at him. 'No, your eyes rolled back.'

She shuddered, and he added coolly, 'Yes. Most unpleasant, I assure you. And quite impossible to fake, I imagine. Your nerves must be shot.'

'Can you wonder why?' Her indignation gave her a welcome shot of adrenalin. 'You pounced on me——'

'I didn't touch you.' He spoke flatly, without emphasis, yet the hurried words died in her throat. 'You've lost weight. Why are you starving yourself?'

'I'm not.'

A sudden gust of anger was communicated by the clenching of his hand on her shoulder. 'Just pining away? For Samuel Darcy? He's recovering slowly from his suicide attempt, but his wife is having a field day. The newspapers love her; she has called you everything from a modern Jezebel to a Salome who danced while her husband's head was up for grabs. She has, however, decided that now you're out of the way she's going back to him.' A hateful cynicism hardened his words. 'He, of course, has the money.'

Alexa felt befouled by the gossip, smirched and degraded, but curiously enough the savage note in his voice didn't add to it. She thought bitterly that, although he was only too ready to believe the worst of her, at least he didn't revel in every salacious detail.

However, she pulled away from his grasp, her voice a thin thread in the great silence of the night. 'I'm glad he's recovering,' she said. 'Poor Sam.'

'You can still say that, after he laid you open to all this speculation and notoriety?'

Stiffly, responding to the contemptuous tone rather than the words, she retorted, 'It wasn't Sam's fault.'

Incredulously he asked, 'Are you in love with the man?'

She drew a deep painful breath and turned her face away. 'That is none of your business.'

He laughed, the sardonic humour biting and savage. 'No, I thought not. Just out for what you can get. A pity you chose the wrong organisation, the wrong man. Sam Darcy is a fool. If you had come to me I'd have known how to look after you. If you want to work there are plenty of ways to satisfy your ambition without pushing you so far and so fast that you were bound to attract undesirable publicity. Unfortunately, you're too notorious now for any self-respecting company to employ you. What do you plan to do?'

Sheer feral fury roughened her voice, but the words came clearly, falling like ice drops into the warm air. 'I'm going to do what I should have done before and go back to the bach. I've had my ration of insults for the week, Mr Venetos. Goodnight.'

She pushed herself up on to her feet, but the effect of her defiant words was totally lost as her head spun treacherously again. She gave an involuntary moan as he grabbed her. Beneath the thin material of his shirt sleeve he was pure steel, the muscles moving smoothly as they adjusted to the extra strain of her precipitous lurch against him.

'What is it?' he demanded.

She was white to the lips but she said pugnaciously, 'Nothing.'

The moonlight picked out the strong features as he looked down at her. She straightened up and pulled away, then gasped as he swung her up into his arms.

'Hush,' he said easily. 'The Range Rover is over the brow of the hill. I'll take you home.'

He was incredibly strong, for she was no lightweight and yet he managed to get her to the opulent vehicle with no more signs of fatigue than a slight increase in the rate of his breathing. Alexa found the short walk up the hill totally unnerving. She too was the victim of a vastly speeded-up breathing rate, but it was not due to effort. She was disturbed to realise that she found it extremely erotic to be held so easily in his arms, to be carried as though she was small and fragile. He was sweating slightly, and she had to stiffen herself against leaning her head on his shoulder, against looping her arms across those broad shoulders and relaxing into mindless acquiescence.

This, she thought, was why women had pretended for aeons to be the weaker sex. It was shameful and degrading, yet powerfully seductive. No wonder so many women surrendered to the potent instinct to give up their independence for the protection of some male because he offered a security that appealed to their most primitive needs and desires.

Oh, Leon Venetos was a very attractive male, all charisma, with an animal magnetism rendered even more potent by the fact that he was intelligent, but Alexa knew enough to realise that it was not his brilliant intellect that was making her breath drag shallowly through her lungs. She was the victim of one of Nature's little jokes, the blind, impartial instinct to reproduce, more powerful than anything else because it was programmed into her genes.

The fact that he thought her little better than a slut meant nothing against this sort of desire. Mind and logic warred with instinct, and the dark hunger won.

But it could be controlled by the force of will and reason.

She said nothing beyond a brief word of thanks when he put her into the front seat, lacing her fingers together so hard that the knuckles showed white in the dimness as he swung around the front of the vehicle and into the seat behind the wheel.

He drove as smoothly as he could across the paddocks and down the track to the bach. Alexa cast one look at the chiselled profile, all hard angles and straight lines except for the curve of his mouth, then looked hurriedly away. He was remote and cold and unreachable.

Once there, he carried her inside in spite of her protests and deposited her on the floor in the living-room, asking curtly, 'Will you be all right?'

The light lingered blue in the depths of her hair as she nodded. 'Yes.' It was all she intended to say, but as he turned away the good manners instilled by her parents forced more words from her. 'I should thank you...'

At once the concern vanished, to be replaced by a smile that was at once derisive and without humour. 'Oh, you will,' he said softly, his eyes on the sweet curve of her mouth. 'I'll see that you do.'

It sounded so much like a threat that she took a step back, and had to grab at a chair to support herself. She swallowed hard as images rose to her mind of his hands on her skin, dark against its pallor in her most secret places...

Fiercely she banished them, but he looked at her from half-closed eyes gleaming beneath heavy lids, and a smile curled the corners of that hard, beautiful mouth.

'Not yet,' he said, calmly, evenly. 'Not yet, Alexa. But soon, I promise you.'

She watched him go, striding lithely back to the Range Rover and wondered bleakly if it was that air of complete assurance which made him so attractive. How did the physical components of his body, however perfect, lean legs and narrow hips, the strength embodied in muscle and sinew and long bones, the poise of a head—how did they knit together in this one man to project such an intangible quality as disciplined masculine authority, forceful and formidable?

And why should it be this man, of all men, who had the power to make her heart beat so heavily in her breast that the sound of the waves was drowned out entirely?

When the noise of the vehicle had died away she went into the bedroom and collapsed on to the bed. Why had he made that last promise—or was it a threat? Did he really mean it, or had it amused him to make her sweat it out, and wonder feverishly how she would stop herself from falling shamefully into his arms if he really followed up the attraction that sizzled between them?

By morning she had made up her mind that she was not going to worry any more about Leon Venetos. Not a bit. Not ever again. She was going to banish him from her mind. Armed with this decision, she went out on to the terrace and curled up in a chair with a good book and the crosswords.

She hadn't been there more than ten minutes when the Range Rover drove up. In spite of herself her heart gave a lurch, but settled down as a feminine figure climbed briskly out and came across the long grass.

Her visitor was about twenty-three or -four, small and voluptuously built, with surprisingly long legs. As she swayed towards her, Alexa saw that she was beautiful in a red-lipped, long-lashed way, even when she looked angry, as she did.

'You are Alexa Severn?' She had a little-girl voice with a pretty English accent.

Warily, Alexa agreed that that was who she was.

The pale eyes surveyed her very comprehensively. Then the woman nodded. 'I see,' she said softly.

With somewhat of a snap Alexa returned, 'I'm afraid I don't.'

'No?' An eyebrow went up. 'You are beautiful, but more than that, you are a little out of the common way. All of Leon Venetos's mistresses are. He is not a man who enjoys ordinary women.'

'Quite possibly.' Alexa's voice was starkly angry. 'But I'm not his mistress.'

'Perhaps not now, but you will be. Otherwise, why would he be getting rid of me?'

Alexa pushed a hand across her eyes, wondering if the woman was slightly deranged. 'I'm sorry?'

The newcomer stood leaning against a column, staring out to sea. When she spoke it was in a flat little voice, as though she was reining in emotions too great to be borne. 'It's a thing he has. He is faithful. At least, for as long as it lasts. He won't sleep with another woman until he gets rid of the current one. Rather admirable, isn't it, in this day of elastic morals? However, when it's over, that's it, you're out. He's not at all sentimental. I suspected that something was wrong when he brought you back to the homestead and wouldn't let me anywhere near you, but he seemed to relax after you had been dispatched here.'

Alexa said wearily, 'You're quite wrong, you know.'

'I saw the way he looked at you out on the veranda. Oh, yes,' at Alexa's astonishment, 'I was there, just around the corner. I slept in the next room. It's another thing Leon has. He never sleeps with his women.'

She sounded tolerantly amused, as though his foibles were easily endured. To her profound astonishment and dismay Alexa found herself thinking that if Leon was her lover she would be furious if he slept in another bed.

The other woman went on, 'He gave me emeralds for Christmas. Beautiful... But since you stayed the night, he hasn't been near me. And then he came in this morning, and told me it was over. Oh, he was pleasant, and kind, but merciless. So I thought I'd come across this morning and check out my supplanter.'

Alexa was appalled. 'Do you mean he just dumped you, dismissed you like—like...?'

The woman gave her a lopsided smile. 'Like a discarded mistress, is the correct term,' she said softly. 'Yes, just like that. That's how he'll dump you, too, when he finds the next woman he wants. Oh, he'll make sure you understand the rules, right at the start, but the trouble is that occasionally one of us forgets them and starts hoping that she'll be the one to tame him.'

Alexa was sickened by this, her expression one of cold disgust. The younger woman laughed softly, drearily.

'It happens,' she said. 'We women are stupidly at the mercy of our hearts, whereas Leon hasn't got one. But he's a superb lover, generous and exciting, the only man I've ever had who can make me want him just by smiling. Not that that's all he can do—heaven knows where he learned them, but he's got tricks that I'd never come across before, not even in the Kama Sutra. Enjoy him for as long as he has you, and always remember that it won't last forever, and that way you'll get off without anything more than a dented heart and a technique in bed that'll thrill your next lover. As well as a collection of whatever insurance you want for your old age. He's very generous, when he's pleased. Goodbye, Miss Severn.'

Alexa watched dumbly as she undulated back to the Range Rover. She was not in the least puzzled by the other woman's motives. Lady Whoever-she-was had come partly out of curiosity but more to do as much damage to a relationship she didn't know to be non-existent. But in spite of the malice, there had been genuine pain there too, and Alexa felt sorry for her.

And renewed anger with Leon Venetos. Mixed in with the anger was fear, for in spite of the very logical processes of her brain she knew she was more than susceptible to the fierce virile magnetism he projected so effortlessly. However, she thought calmly, he wouldn't rape her, so all she had to do was learn to keep detached and guard her unawakened body and all should be well.

She didn't fool herself that it would be easy. The Alexa of a few weeks ago would have laughed at the thought of any man overcoming her innate reserve by the sheer force of his virility, but she was much more cautious now. Whereas once she had been a little contemptuous of those women who wailed that they hadn't been able to help themselves, that they were overcome by passion, she now had more respect for the forces that could banish self-respect and control. For the first time she thought she understood the compulsion that had brought her mother all the way from London to the island.

The American couple returned with two large cartons of groceries; they stayed long enough to drink a cup of coffee and then left for another landfall further up the coast. She waved them goodbye with real regret, wondering wistfully if she could enjoy a life like that, following the sunsets and the next long wave to wherever it took her.

No, she needed a home, a settled place. She began to think seriously about what she should do with her life now, how she wanted to be living for the next twenty years.

Fainting at Leon Venetos's feet convinced her that it was stupid not to eat, so she made herself three small meals during the day, and she had to admit that she was feeling better for them.

She spent the morning on the terrace and the afternoon inside in the cool, working her way through the cryptic crosswords she had bought, easing the turmoil in her heart by concentrating so furiously that she got through them far too fast.

But when, as the sky was turning soft pink and gold, she heard the sound of the Range Rover, she knew that she had been waiting, and for the first time she wondered if she was going to be able to resist Leon Venetos.

It should be easy. He was everything she despised in a man. So why was her breath coming quickly through

lips that had parted on a sigh of delight? And what was
the sudden pang in the pit of her stomach?

He came up from the beach, walking as though he
owned the world and everything in it, the sun gleaming
gold on that thick hair. Such unusual colouring, Alexa
thought, trying desperately to be objective. The opposite of her own; she had dark hair and blue eyes and
a skin that was palest gold, whereas in spite of that pale
hair he tanned well, and his eyes were the stormy grey
of a thundercloud.

Dwelling on his physical attributes was not the way to
keep her self-possession, so she dragged her eyes away
from the broad shoulders and the dusting of hair that
scrolled in an antique pattern over the wide, tanned chest
and down to the waistband of his old denim shorts.
Adonis stalking a nymph, she thought hollowly, as her
pulses beat an erratic little rhythm throughout her body.

He didn't hurry. He strolled towards her with an arrogant air of authority, looking around him at the serene
waters of the little cove, the smooth, shining sand newly
swept by the day's tide, and the rugged old pohutukawa
trees still crimson and scarlet with their strange fringed
flowers. By the time he got up to the terrace Alexa's
nerves were as taut as wires.

'Good evening,' he said, eyeing with every appearance of enjoyment the length of her legs. 'I'm sorry
I wasn't here sooner, but I had one or two things to do.'

His massive arrogance stung her into an unwise reply.
'Like getting rid of a discarded mistress? What did you
do? Give her a cheque for services rendered and put her
on the first flight back to England?'

His dark brows drew together in a quick frown and
the stern mouth hardened. 'As it happens, she wanted

to stop off at Hawaii on the way home. Who told you about her?'

Well, it couldn't harm the woman, she was already gone, and it might make him realise that Alexa knew what sort of man he was. Shrugging, she said, 'She came around to see me this morning. She seemed to have some strange idea that I was supplanting her in your...' she paused, her voice investing the next and final word with blistering scorn '...affections.'

It had not been a sensible comment to make. He stood looking down at her, the elegantly carved features hard as stone, while a frighteningly savage little smile played around his mouth. In that moment Alexa understood why and how he had managed to parlay his inheritance into an organisation that spoke on terms of equality with governments.

He looked—all power, all bruising naked force. She couldn't prevent the swift indrawn breath, or the involuntary little movement that pressed the support of the lounger hard and painfully into her shoulders.

But she recovered quickly enough. He was not the sort of man to turn protective when confronted by fear; he looked as though that reaction sent him straight to the jugular. So she lifted her head, held her gaze steady, and waited.

His lashes drooped, hiding any sign of emotion in the dark eyes. The dangerous smile deepened as he bent forward and ran a casual, insulting hand from her knee up the long golden length of her thigh. 'As if you hadn't known,' he said, and his fingers tightened on the smooth skin.

His touch burned like fire, like acid, yet apart from that final grip it had moved lightly, almost lovingly over her. Looking down helplessly at the contrast of lean, dark fingers against her skin, Alexa was shaken by a primal awareness so powerful that for a moment she almost went under.

The dangerous challenge in his smile turned to satisfaction. But before he had time to speak she wrested back control from her treacherous senses and said between her teeth, 'I do not want to become your mistress, Mr Venetos. Sensible though I am of the honour you do me, I have an objection to being bought and sold.'

He raised his brows and stood up, his eyes resting almost thoughtfully on her taut white face. 'You do the selling,' he pointed out in a reasonable tone. 'If I didn't know you were on the market I wouldn't insult you by making an offer. Does the thought of being known to be my mistress worry you? I'm afraid I'm not as easily persuaded as Sam Darcy, or as worried about my personal image. I have no wife to be deceived. I don't want you working in my organisation, pretending to be an executive. While you're with me you'll act as my hostess if I need you, and keep my bed warm.'

Something heated and feral kindled in his gaze. Once more Alexa shrank back, every nerve tightening.

He laughed and came down beside her on the lounger. 'In fact, I may never let you out of my bed,' he said beneath his breath, and bent and kissed her, his mouth hard and urgent, blotting out everything but the taste and scent and feel of him in all his dark male sorcery.

In spite of her promise to herself to stay in command Alexa felt herself go under. The pressure of his mouth, the sudden wild leap of response that thrilled through her completely overthrew the common sense she had tried to use as a defence. Hating herself, yet unable to resist, she sank beneath the controlled hunger of his desire, making no protest as he deepened the kiss into an intimacy that should have had her screaming for help.

If she could have got a scream around his kiss, that was. But Alexa wasn't thinking about anything but the tide of passion that was rising through her body, pulling at her sinews and muscles until her body was racked with it. She was aching as though she had a fever, tensely straining towards some unknown goal.

'Gently,' Leon whispered, a note of lazy laughter warming his voice. 'Such enthusiasm is flattering, but I prefer to take my pleasures slowly, easily, because that way I appreciate the final satisfaction so much more.'

His hand slid from her chin to the long column of her throat, the fingers gliding sensuously down, creating spirals and ripples of fire through her body. She gasped, as those knowing, experienced fingers found the pulse that throbbed there, then resumed the mesmerising journey across the fine bones of her shoulder before coming to rest on the first smooth swell of her breast.

More than anything in the world she wanted him to continue; more than life or honour or self-respect she needed to feel the touch of his hand on her breast. Already she was conscious of the stiffening of her muscles there, the unfamiliar heaviness and heat, the almost imperceptible yet so vividly felt peaking of each nipple beneath the soft white cotton of her shirt.

Strange tides of sensation swirled through her body; strange contradictory longings ached in her bones. She wanted to feel his hand touch her delicately, she wanted to pull him down on top of her so that his weight crushed her into the lounger...

His breath on her lips was erotic. Heavy, drugged lashes moved upwards; he was smiling, the grey of his gaze lit from behind by a satisfaction so intense it was like flames in his eyes.

'Ask me, Alexa,' he said silkily. 'Tell me what you like. Tell me what you want. Whatever it is, I'll give it to you.'

It sounded like the temptation offered by a supremely sophisticated devil, promising every sensual delight in exchange for her soul.

Alexa's hands clenched into fists as she fought a battle more important than any other in her life, a battle *for* her life, she thought hazily. It was so hard to stem the red tide of passion, to quench it with the knowledge that all that he wanted of her was the temporary use of her body, whereas she had everything to lose, her pride, her dignity, her heart.

Grittily, the swift colour fleeing her skin, she managed to say, 'I don't want this.'

She expected anger, perhaps scorn, but not the laughter that was his response. 'No?' he drawled, narrow-eyed and mocking. 'Then why are these asking for my hand— and my mouth?'

His fingers brushed the hardened sensitised tip of one breast; watching her with a taunting smile, he moved his hand to the other, rubbing the palm slowly back and forth so lightly that only her skin knew what he had done.

Sensation, fierce as fire, rapturous as ecstasy, sizzled through her body. She couldn't stop the tiny gasp that escaped her lips, but she retained enough self-control to reach out and throw his hand away as though his touch burned.

'You want me,' he said harshly. 'Just as much as I want you. We can make excuses, say anything we like to save our pride, but the body never lies. Look.'

He caught her hand and held it against him, and she gave a hoarse little cry and wrenched her hand free, staring at him with dilated, terrified eyes.

'It works both ways,' he said deeply, frowning slightly at her reaction. 'I can't hide it from you, either. But I'm damned if I'm going to play games with you. Sam Darcy might be turned on by coy pseudo-virginal teasing, but I'm not. I like honest responses to an honest desire.'

CHAPTER FOUR

SHE was desperate to get rid of him, but some innate instinct warned her that she would have to tread warily. She didn't know how to deal with a pirate who saw no shame in admitting to and accepting sexual passion.

Not that he was as controlled as he seemed to be. A swift glance revealed that the darkness of his irises had engulfed the pupils of his eyes and a heated band of colour crawled along his high, fierce cheekbones. If she really antagonised him, who knew what he might do, especially as her response had been so unrestrained and unequivocal.

She didn't know how to cope, so in the end she decided on honesty. 'My body is not me,' she said with difficulty. She had never spoken so freely before, and her tongue felt too big for her mouth. 'I—I don't want to—to put myself in hock to an emotion that I'm not proud of, that I resent. You must know that any—any attractive man and woman can feel a—desire for each other. It's normal and natural—the urge to perpetuate the species. But I don't want to give in to it.'

'Why not?' He spoke softly, so she didn't look up at him, aware that he tested her resolution too much. Tenderness could well be the one thing she couldn't resist.

'Because I—because you can't just snatch what you want. I want to fall...'

Self-preservation stopped the betraying words before she had time to finish them, but that he had understood was only too plain. She stirred wretchedly at the open mockery in his laughter, but remained pressed back against the lounger. Something warned her that she was in great danger.

'Are you trying to tell me that you were in love with Sam Darcy?' he asked at last, not trying to hide the incredulous note in his voice.

Before she could think she shook her head.

'No, I thought not,' he said sardonically. 'Presumably you slept with him because he promised to help you get where you wanted to go. I'm not so stupid. I'll give you anything within reason that you want, but I'm not having my business reputation sent down the drain by thinking with my gonads.'

'You really are a chauvinist,' she said acidly. 'Don't you employ women in this precious business of yours?'

'Oh, I do, but I make damned sure they are there to work, not to play executive in return for the loan of their pretty bodies,' he returned, smiling mirthlessly.

Alexa's eyes blazed. His closeness, the heat from his body, suffocated her. In a sudden need to be free she swung off the lounger and on to the terrace. 'Get out!' she snapped, colour gathering in two patches over her cheekbones. 'Go home!'

'Certainly, but you're coming home with me.'

She gasped. 'You're crazy! I wouldn't go home with you if you begged me to!'

He got to his feet and stood looking down at her, the light of battle and something else, an enigmatic satisfaction, gleaming in his eyes. 'I wouldn't beg you for my life,' he said silkily. 'But you're coming home with me because there's a tropical cyclone on the way down from the Islands.'

Her eyes flashed to the calm serenity of the sky, then back to his face. She had endured a cyclone when she was a child, and she remembered it vividly. But aloud she argued, 'I'll be perfectly safe here. The bach is sheltered from——'

'Don't be a fool,' he said tersely. 'I'm not leaving you here alone. They've got cyclone warnings out for all the North Island, and from what they're saying it's going to be a big one. You're coming home with me if I have to gag and tie you up.'

'But usually they peter out before they get here. It's ridiculous to... Where are you going?'

'To pack.'

She hurtled after his long-legged stride into the bedroom, shouting, 'Get out! Leave my things alone!'

'Alexa,' he said gently, opening the wardrobe doors, 'shut up.'

A little demon of fear unfolded its wings in her throat. She realised that she wasn't prepared to force the issue. Sullenly, her eyes so furious that the blue was closer to ultramarine, she said, 'All right, damn you, I'll pack.'

He gave her an ironic, unrepentant grin, then disappeared into the rest of the house. He moved so quietly that she didn't hear his footsteps, she had to judge what he was doing by the sounds of the refrigerator door being opened and shut, then the soft hiss of the sliding doors as they were closed.

Within five minutes he was back, his smile an open taunt at the mutiny of her expression. 'You look pretty when you're angry,' he said, as he picked up the suitcase.

Alexa was so furious that she could barely breathe, but something about the way he spoke made her lips twitch. She tried to smother the laughter but it bubbled free, oddly evocative, a choked gurgle that made her realise just how rarely she had laughed lately.

'Now that's a sound I'd like to hear more of,' he said encouragingly.

Her amusement ebbed and died. 'Not many people enjoy being kidnapped. Or accused of selling themselves to climb higher up the corporate ladder.'

'Enjoy the kidnapping as a new experience. As for the other—if you can't stand the heat, be grateful that I'm pulling you out of the kitchen,' he said coolly. 'Now that you understand that I'm not amenable to that sort of persuasion, we should have no difficulty in reaching an understanding.'

For as long as I still want to go to bed with you.

He didn't say the words, but the implication was blatant and insulting. Alexa wondered drearily how it was possible to hate someone yet be rapturously, totally aware of them, to feel a need that was painful and ecstatic at the same time. It seemed unfair that it should happen just now, when she had so much else to worry about.

She said curtly, 'What else should we be doing? If the cyclone ever gets this far...' She looked around, noting that he had brought in all the outdoor furniture and fastened the bolt across the doors.

'We'll tape the windows,' he said, producing a large roll of tape.

It didn't take long, but it was oddly pleasant to be working with him, even though she was worried about the welfare of the bach. However, another glance outside revealed a sky as innocent and calm as a Madonna's robe, so she relaxed. Cyclones were not common; as she had said, most of them died out in the vast regions of the Pacific north of New Zealand. If this wasn't a false alarm, it would probably only turn out to be a summer storm.

Once inside the Range Rover he looked at her for a moment before turning the key, his eyes very keen and searching but enigmatic. He had the face of a poker player, impassive, almost indolent, yet there was that impression of great alertness. It had to be a great help in the sort of life he led.

'Try to relax. It won't,' he said with a hateful, and probably entirely spurious, air of reason, 'do you any harm to take some time out. I presume that's why you came here in the first place, to lick your wounds and make some decisions. I'll see that you don't lose by it.'

'Don't,' she said in a voice that was hoarse with feeling, 'don't you dare offer me money.'

'Offend your sense of propriety?' His raised brows were speculative. 'Do you want the pretty lying words? They only seem to make a straightforward arrangement less . . .'

'Commercial?'

He reacted to the single word with a frown. 'Hardly commercial.' And leaned over so that she could see the grain of his skin, fine and exotically different from the smooth satin of her own. A knowing little smile quirked his mouth as her eyes widened. Nervously she touched lips that were suddenly dry with her tongue, then cursed herself as his eyes kindled at the tiny betrayal.

'This,' he said softly, just above her mouth, 'is far from commercial, Alexa. You're trying to fight it by pretending that it is so, but you'll fail because, in spite of yourself, you cannot resist the challenge. Is this the first time you've encountered such a need? Have all of your previous lovers been buyers of that delectable body only? Somehow I find it hard to believe that you have been untouched by sensuality. Your response is that of a passionate woman. This time there will be no *quid pro quo*. You will grace my bed because that is where you want to be. And you will accept my loving because that will be payment enough.'

'You're damned conceited,' she said, but her voice was trembling.

'Ah, it frightens you. But then, before you've always been the one in command, the one who dispenses the favours. Not this time, Alexa. This time you will learn how it is to be the one who receives, the supplicant. I have seen how the desire for you can turn a man like Sam Darcy into a suicide. That is not going to happen to me.'

When he was angry or passionate, when that massive control slipped, he spoke with a faint hint of not so much an accent as a different intonation, that reminded her that his father had been an Italian immigrant. She heard it now, and as her eyes widened at the sheer cold purposefulness in his voice she saw that a muscle beside his mouth jerked twice, then was still.

His words chilled her blood. They promised degradation and a loss of self-respect so intense that she knew she would never recover from it.

Did he really mean what he had said? Or had anger made him lose control? She said nothing, but her expression must have given her away, because he smiled and touched her mouth with his, softly, in a kiss that should have been tender, but was an act of power.

She flinched back and he lifted his head, frowning. 'What is the matter?'

'Nothing.' Her voice was stifled and uneven. 'But I don't want to become your mistress. And if you force me it will be rape.'

He said cynically, 'I will not have to force you.'

'Rape need not be physical.' She spoke fervently, the words carefully chosen, deliberate. 'I admit that——'

'That you want me.'

'Yes. But if you use that to take me, when you know that I am unwilling, that is rape. Oh, you will probably be able to make me enjoy it, I can see that you're very experienced, but I shall hate myself afterwards, and I shall hate you, too.'

He didn't like that. He sat back and surveyed her, and for the first time since they had met there was an unwilling respect in his face even though his mouth was twisted. 'You're quick to pick up on a man's weakness,' he said after a moment. He switched the engine on and said crisply, 'I suppose it's essential in the life you've chosen. So, you win. I shall wait until you admit to yourself that the real reason for your objection is that you like to be in control, and this time you have no excuse for making love but that you want me.'

Exhausted, she gave up trying to convince him that he was wrong. She had won herself time, and provided he didn't force the issue she would be safe. She was never likely to give him the surrender he expected; it was only in his arms that she became witless and shamefully bereft of control. Away from them she retained her self-control.

All she had to do was make sure that he kept his distance, and she was prepared to use the reluctant concession she had extracted to do it.

It didn't occur to her to wonder how she knew he could be trusted.

The track over the hill to Homestead Bay had a bad surface but he drove skilfully and the Range Rover was comfortable, built to deal with more than that easily. At the top of the hill she looked around, and leaned forward, her face intent and interested as she looked further up into the hills in the interior. The sun was setting in a glory of scarlet and gold, the long rays emphasising the rows and rows of tiny trees that covered the steep faces in the interior of the island.

'You've done a lot of planting,' she said. 'What are you planning to do with the island?'

'That is none of your business. You gave up any claim to the rest of the island when your father sold it.'

It was a direct rebuff. She said shortly, 'I know,' looking away to hide the sudden tears that gleamed beneath her lashes.

He stopped the vehicle, switching off the engine. His voice was reflective, cool and with a faint hint of astonishment, as though he was surprised to find himself giving an explanation. 'I want to return the island to a more natural state, and the first thing to do is plant the hills in some approximation of the *taraire* forest that would have been its natural cover before some idiot burned it all.'

'My great-great-great-grandfather,' she acknowledged wryly. 'He didn't intend to, of course. Like the rest of the pioneers he cut down the bush on all the easy country, but, unlike most of them, he didn't see the forest as an enemy. He wanted to leave all the steepest faces still forested, and he felt that a thick fringe of bush around the island would shelter it from the worst of the winds. Unfortunately, although he took all the precautions he could, a gale sprang up when he was firing and burnt the whole island to a crisp, apart from the pohutukawas on the cliffs. Family tradition has it that he never ceased mourning the loss of the big trees.'

She turned her head to look down over the bay, her eyes remote as they surveyed the white homestead and the other buildings there, the way the approaching night pooled around the buildings like a mist, rendering them romantically mysterious. A hawk did his last lazy, predatory swoop over the hills, grace and danger in the indolent rise and fall of its flight. Alexa shivered as it folded its wings and dropped like a stone to the ground. She knew the sensation of being hunted by a pitiless enemy.

Leon's voice only added to her unease. 'Why did your father sell?'

She shrugged, remembering the pain of those days, the sense of betrayal. 'When he and my mother separated he had to sell the place. She was entitled to half of the assets.'

'I see.'

'Yes. The law's been changed so it doesn't happen that way now, but then...' She paused, her face sad. 'Sometimes I think that my mother forced the issue to punish him. My father loved the island and she loved him, but she couldn't live happily here.'

'A not uncommon story. One must marry the life-style as well as the man. Where is she now?'

She stiffened. 'In London,' she said neutrally.

'And your father?'

'He bought another station with his share, miles from anywhere on the volcanic plateau. He and his second wife live there.'

'How old were you when your parents divorced?'

There was no reason not to answer, but she felt uneasy, as though she was giving away secrets. 'Fifteen,' she said, after a moment's hesitation.

'And did you go with your mother?'

'No. I was at boarding school so they left me there.'

'Poor child.'

Her shoulders moved in the smallest of shrugs. She didn't want him to be sympathetic. 'It happens,' she said, infusing her voice with indifference. 'What sort of childhood did you have?'

He laughed softly, as though he understood her reason for turning the tables and was amused by it. 'Very happy. My parents were well suited, and loved each other until the day my father died. I think my mother loves him still.'

'You were lucky,' she said on a snap. 'Looks, money, power and a happy childhood too. Do you ever wonder if luck has to be paid for?'

'Occasionally,' he said, smiling at her astonished glance. 'It has occurred to me. However, I refuse to allow things over which I have no control to affect my pleasure in life. I work hard, I use my money wisely, I intend to choose a wife who will be as loving to me as my mother was to my father—I can do no more to ward off evil.'

The thought of his marriage gave her heart a strange little tweak. To hide it she said with cool amusement, 'You sound like a fatalist.'

'No. Far from it. Are you?'

'No.' Her brow wrinkled as she said slowly, 'I believe in luck, but I think it has less influence on our lives than, say, willpower. And I think that most of what happens to us is caused by our own actions. Or the lack of them.'

He nodded, putting the vehicle into motion again. 'I find myself agreeing. How long has it been since you were here last?'

The abrupt change of subject threw her for a moment, but she followed his lead. 'Not since I was fifteen.'

'And you are...?'

She smiled. 'I'm twenty-eight,' she said with irony. 'How old are you?'

'Thirty-four.'

She nodded. He looked about that, but the air of authority that was an inherent part of the man made him seem older. Until he smiled, and then she saw the man who had grown up in a happy home with parents who adored him.

He was smiling now, the arrogant profile silhouetted against the brilliant blue of the channel. Alexa dragged her eyes away and looked down at the homestead complex, noting again without surprise the signs of the vast amounts of money which had poured into it, from the newly planked jetty to the concrete helipad, complete with helicopter.

'Are you planning to keep it as a working station?' she asked.

He shot her a sideways glance, piercing as a rapier, but said in a non-committal tone, 'For the moment, yes. I enjoy my holidays here.'

Which probably meant he had plans he wasn't admitting to.

She watched dreamily as they came down through the hill and along between the oleander bushes, wondering how she could read him so well when all she knew about him was that he was a bastard with an exotic taste in mistresses and a ruthless attitude.

At the door he stopped the engines and came around to her door. The last rays of the dying sun gleamed like tawny fire in his hair.

Alexa felt as though she was shutting the door on her past life as he took her into the morning-room where they had eaten breakfast the morning of her arrival on the island.

There was a strangely formal note in his voice as he suggested she sit down. 'I must see that everything is being done. I'll be back shortly and I'll take you up to your room then.'

He didn't wait for her answer, and she was subsiding back on to the cushions when Chris Venetos came in. He stopped, staring at her, and then a knowing smile curled his mouth. 'Well, well, well,' he murmured as he advanced into the room, 'that didn't take long.'

Alexa's mouth hardened into a straight line. 'Your brother brought——'

'Naturally!'

'. . . brought me here because of this cyclone.'

'Not because of your legs?' He inspected them both, taking his time. Stunned, Alexa stared at him.

'I'd have brought you here because of your legs,' he said politely, beginning the same assessment of her other assets.

It was easy to see that he wanted to shock. Alexa sighed. 'Don't you think you're a little young to be sizing up the merchandise quite so blatantly?'

He contrived to grin and look offended at the same time. 'I'll have you know I learned that look in the cradle. We Venetos men are famed for it.'

'Well, if you don't mind, I'd just as soon you didn't try it on me. I'm not accustomed to it and I don't like it.'

His grin twisted. 'Oh, you won't have to worry about me trying to poach on my brother's preserves,' he assured her with an uncomfortable sophistication. 'I know better than to think I'd have any luck. Leon is very definitely the boss in this family. I've never been able to measure up and I've given up trying. And although he's pretty generous as a brother he's not into sharing his ladies around. So just remember, you start to look elsewhere and you'll be down the road so fast you won't know what's hit you.'

Alexa said frigidly, 'When I become your brother's mistress I'll remember that. In the meantime, I can do without either the leers or the handy hints on how to behave, thank you.'

'Leers? I never leer! That was a perfectly normal look when confronted by a raving beauty!' He laughed, although it faded when Leon came back into the room. In fact, he looked guilty and ill-at-ease. 'Oh, hi. I was just commiserating with, ah—Alexa, over her sore knee,' he said, flushing a little under his brother's sapient eye.

'I didn't know that Alexa had a sore knee.'

Apparently that blighting tone was familiar. Chris said very swiftly, 'Well, I'll see you both later,' and slid out of the room in a manner strongly suggestive of an eel.

An eel, Alcxa decided thoughtfully and in some amusement, with just the faintest hint of a swagger.

Leon looked down at her using his height to intimidate as he said with icy clarity, 'My brother will be here for a couple of days. Try not to lure him too far into the realms of calf-love, if you please. He has no power to give you any sort of position in the organisation!'

She clamped down hard on her anger, satisfying her pride by saying in her coolest, most remote voice, 'I'm not looking for a position in your organisation, thank you.'

'Just as well, because I'm not making one for you.'

In a calm voice, investing the words with a scorn so delicate it took a perceptive ear to discern it, she said, 'You are so arrogant it comes treacherously close to vanity. What makes you think that I want anything to do with you?'

'This.'

His mouth was hard and possessive, almost brutal. Just as brutal was the fire that fountained through her at the kiss. Even more brutal was the effort she needed to maintain her self-control. She sat with her neck stretched back and forced her mouth to stay passive and unwelcoming beneath the onslaught, calling on such reserves of strength that she was exhausted by the effort.

At last he took his mouth from hers, watching through narrowed eyes as the blood rushed back into her lips. His thumb traced the line of them, gently, almost as though he cherished the soft flesh. His expression was mask-like. If it hadn't been for the slivers of hot grey beneath his long lashes she would have thought that he was totally unaffected by that kiss.

'You intrigue me,' he murmured. 'And frustrate me. But that's no excuse for bruising you. I'm not normally a violent lover.'

Something very odd happened in Alexa's stomach. She resented the fact that her stupid body had this weakness where he was concerned, but this was not the usual spark of desire. At that moment she had a momentary vision, a kind of sharp, vivid image of him bending over her in a huge bed, his face taut with an intolerable need. She saw the lean darkness of his hand, strangely barbaric against the soft white skin of her breast. She saw roses, darkly red, and the pale shimmer of satin, and a wild flamenco guitar driving the air to madness and frenzy...

The glittering darkness of his eyes, so close to hers, seemed to swallow her up. She felt a flood of heat through her body, electricity running through her nerves, and with it, overpowering it, a rich sensual need like honey and fire.

He saw it. He smiled, slowly, almost cruelly, and then the tawny-gold head dipped and he kissed her again. Her arms wound around his neck, her hands splayed out across the breadth of his back. She felt the play of muscles there, and she wanted more than anything to be able to run her hands across his naked skin, and know that there was nothing between them.

'You taste of wild flowers,' he said into her mouth. 'You feel like silk warmed in the sun. Would it be so difficult to forget your pride and let all this happen?'

The deep, slightly thickened timbre made her shudder. Her lips felt slack and cold as she said, 'Yes.'

'Why?'

'Because I——' No, she couldn't tell him that if she slept with him, if she lay in his arms and learned what it was like to live her woman's role to the full, she would never be free of him. If he learned how defenceless she was he would use her weakness as a weapon, and she didn't know what she would do when he tired of her and she was alone once more. Aloud, wearily, she said, 'Because there's no future in it. Because I don't want to.'

She had betrayed herself. She saw a flash of comprehension lighten his scrutiny. 'You're afraid,' he said softly, savouring the words.

'No.'

He laughed, his eyes resting on the rapid shallow pulsing at the base of her throat. 'Yes, you are. What are you afraid of, Alexa? That for once in your life you might forget to use your body as a bargaining counter? That you might give in to the hidden desires you have sublimated up until now?'

He had never seemed so dangerous before. It was radiating from him, an aura of alert suspicion, apparent for only a second before he dampened it down and she could no longer see anything beyond the handsome surface. A kind of disappointment flooded through her, banishing all but a trace of the sensual appreciation of a moment ago. For a few moments they had communicated fully, a man and a woman in each other's arms. Now they were enemies once more.

'Why not trust me?' he asked, his voice very deep, very persuasive.

The cynical note of her laughter banished any softness from his expression. 'I'd as soon trust a snake,' she said caustically. 'However, I'll make a bargain with you.'

'No bargains.'

'You might find this one interesting. I'll trust you when you trust me. Isn't that supposed to be how truly equal relationships work?'

He stood up and moved away from her, his expression revealing nothing but a sardonic amusement. 'I don't want a truly equal relationship with you,' he said cruelly. 'In fact, I don't want a relationship at all. I want you. That's all.'

'Am I supposed to be flattered because the great Leon Venetos wants me?' She wanted the question to ring with scorn, but it came out flat with weariness.

'Why should you be? I'm just a man, no better and no worse than any other man. If it flatters you to know that I want you, then go ahead, be flattered. However, I imagine that you've had enough men look at you with desire in your life to have lost any inclination to foolish coyness.' He touched her hair, an oddly gentle gesture for a man who was propositioning her in the crudest terms. 'Passion is a fact of life. It's only when it becomes tangled up with other things that it becomes sordid. I'm offering you the means to gratify a very pleasant, uncomplicated need.'

She almost believed him, but as she looked up, her eyes heavy with doubt, she saw something else in the angular features, a kind of driven hunger which made her realise that for once in his life Leon was deluding himself. Whatever he was offering her, it was not the simple gratification of desire. There were darker undertones to it, ones she could sense if not understand.

Yet his fingers were gentle through the heavy warm silk of her hair, as though he loved the feel of it. Well, why not? she thought robustly, trying to escape a delicious lassitude that welled up from deep inside her. Leon was a very sensual man. That stark animal magnetism was one of the first things that she had noticed about him. Virility and a dark masculine strength appealed beyond the rational. There would be few women who could look at him and remain totally unmoved.

She knew of only one other man who had that instant appeal to the senses. Jake Ferrers, who was married to her best friend Cathy. And he, she thought with a wry humour that lifted the corners of her mouth a fraction, had led Cathy a fine dance. Although, to listen to him tell the story, it was Cathy who had done the leading! Still, they had finally come to understand each other. Their marriage was still as passionate and loving as it had ever been.

But she did not want to understand Leon. She wanted to get as far away from him as possible and enjoy a holiday while she made up her mind what she was to do next.

For the first time since her arrival on the island she realised that she was no longer prey to the bitter world-weariness that had dogged her since the scandal broke. Not once. Somehow Leon had banished it as effectively as though he had shattered the shell of self-pity she had been hiding behind.

'And so?' His voice was amused, yet there was an undertone to it that told her that he was not going to give up. Beneath the sophistication there was a ruthless determination that had made him the man he was.

Slowly she shook her head. He smiled, but his eyes promised her a hard fight and one with no rules. 'You'll trust me enough one day,' he said.

She frowned, because it was an odd remark, but at that moment Chris came back in, his alert eyes sparkling as Leon removed his hand from Alexa's head. 'Have you heard the latest weather report?' he demanded eagerly.

Leon shook his head. Chris said, 'Apparently it's definitely heading down here. It could be here within twenty-four hours!'

'It could dissipate and die, too before it reaches us. Most of them do, thank goodness.' Leon's dry rejoinder made Chris's excitement seem somehow very young.

'Well, I hope it gets here. It would be really exciting. I've never been in a cyclone.'

In an even drier tone his brother retorted, 'I hope you never are. They are not occasions of great joy. People quite frequently die in them, and lose vast amounts of money, sometimes even their livelihood.'

Not at all abashed, Chris gazed somewhat wistfully out at the gentle twilight beyond the windows. 'Well, I suppose they do, but not here, surely? The weather office must keep a good eye on them, so no one's taken by surprise. They say there's no danger at the moment, but people should watch the weather carefully. We'd be protected from it mostly, wouldn't we.'

'If it came to the east, yes. Unfortunately, they have a habit of swinging. One of the disadvantages of cyclones is that they don't seem to know the rules.' Leon looked at Alexa. 'It's a bit early in the year, surely?'

She shrugged. 'Yes, when they come it's usually in March, but, as you said, they're unpredictable.'

'Have you ever been in one?'

She smiled at Chris's eager enquiry. 'A few, but most of the time when they get here they're just tropical depressions. There'll be wind and rain but nothing dramatic.'

She slept that night in the cherrywood bed that had been hers on the night of her arrival, and woke up to a still, cloudy morning that spoke of rain to come.

This time she did not go out on to the veranda. By the time Leon knocked she was dressed in a skirt of her favourite raspberry with a paler shirt. She opened the door and greeted him, trying to ignore the approval she saw in his eyes.

'According to the weather office the cyclone is definitely on its way, and although they're pretty guarded, it's clear they expect it to be a bad one.'

'I've been thinking, Leon. If it hits, I should be in the bach. I can't do anything to protect it——'

'You can stay here.' When she opened her mouth to protest he stopped it with a kiss. 'What could you do if you were there? I'd worry if you were there alone.'

'You're not responsible for me,' she said angrily, trying to calm down a surging pulse rate. 'I can look after myself, for heaven's sake!'

'You haven't made a terribly good job of it so far,' he pointed out in a steely, but perfectly pleasant, tone. 'I don't want to hear any more silly suggestions. You're staying here. Come down and have some breakfast.'

She gave him an indignant look, folded her lips tightly to hold back the hot retort that hovered behind them, and preceded him down the stairs.

The breakfast-room was pleasant even on this dull morning. Chris was eating as though his life depended on it, while a radio played softly in the background. As they came in through the door he commanded, 'Quiet, quiet! Listen!'

The announcer's voice was serious, advising boat owners to check their moorings, warning of the possibility of floods, and the desirability of everyone checking the back cover of the telephone directory so that they knew what to do in case of emergency. Alexa listened, her brows drawing together.

As Leon pushed the chair in behind her the weather forecast came on. All three listened carefully. '. . . Northland and the East Cape, strong easterly winds rising to gale force in exposed places, heavy rain and the possibility of floods in low-lying areas . . .'

When it was over Chris said in a voice where foreboding mixed with excitement, 'Well, that sounds as if we're for it.' He looked at his brother. 'What are we going to do?'

'Batten down the hatches. The first thing to do is tie down the helicopter. Then we'll have to see what else needs doing.' He looked across at Alexa, frowning as she ate a piece of toast. 'I'll send someone over to see if we missed anything at the bach.'

On the point of insisting that she could do it she met his implacable gaze, and subsided. 'Thank you,' she said rather stiffly.

He grinned. 'But you'd rather do it yourself. Never mind, you can punish me for being a good neighbour some other time.'

Breakfast was eaten in record time, and then Alexa was left in the morning-room to waste the morning away while all around her people worked to minimise the effects of the cyclone. Her suggestions that she help were met with blunt refusals.

'There's nothing to do,' the housekeeper told her. 'I've got everything under control. You'll be more hindrance than help.'

After wandering around the house she accepted that her help definitely wasn't needed, and went back into the morning-room and sat down. She watched as the wind got up, the ever stronger gusts whipping up the sea into mutinous grey waves that began to thunder even on to that protected shore.

To keep her mind off the coming cyclone and her own inability to do anything useful, she began to doodle on a sheet of paper. After a few minutes her lassitude vanished. With a sure, certain hand she began to set down equations and formulae, so lost in what she was doing that it wasn't until she heard the men's voices outside on the veranda that she realised it was lunchtime. She had time only to stuff the piece of paper beneath a convenient cushion before they came in, wind-whipped and smelling of rain.

Lunch was another hurried meal, and after it the men disappeared again. Alexa got up to clear the table and was found by the housekeeper, who said crisply, 'This is my job, Miss Severn. Mr Venetos would have something very sharp to say to me if he saw you.'

About to describe Mr Venetos's character in pithy terms, Alexa hesitated, then gave in. She said instead, 'There must be something I can do, surely? Ironing, perhaps? I'm rather good at ironing.'

But the housekeeper was not agreeing to that. She didn't say anything, but it was evident that she had put Alexa in exactly the same category as Leon's mistresses, beautiful but useless.

'I'll get you some magazines,' she said, and bustled briskly out to return a few minutes later with a handful. 'The launch is just about here with the newspapers if you're interested,' she told Alexa.

'Yes, I'd like to see one.'

'Then I'll get someone to bring one in.'

The someone was Sean, belligerent and stiff with resentment. Alexa said, 'Thank you,' as he held the folded paper out to her.

He said curtly, 'I should have known that you'd want the boss. Sorry if I put a spoke in your wheel.'

Crisply, her voice very cold and clear, she retorted, 'It may surprise you, but it is definitely time that you understood that even if I were the prostitute you think me, you have no right to rape me.'

He went scarlet. 'I wouldn't have!'

'I wasn't to know that. From where I was, it seemed a distinct possibility.'

He gave her a furious, baffled look and turned on his heel. She heard his defensive voice outside the room and then Leon was in the doorway, looking at her with a cold savagery that made every hair on her body prickle with fear.

'Can't you leave any man alone?' he asked.

CHAPTER FIVE

THE newspaper slid from her lap on to the floor. Sheer, uncontained rage fountained through her. She had to take a deep breath before she could speak, and even then her voice trembled.

'You are a fool,' she said.

'I rather think I might be.' But he didn't apologise, merely stood looking down at her with something like bitter resentment.

She met his eyes defiantly, unable to work out what he was thinking, and he stooped and picked up the paper, handing it back to her with a twisted excuse for a smile.

But half-way there he stopped, the smile disappearing. His brows twitched together as he stared at something on the page.

Then he handed it over, his face icily controlled. 'Gloating, were you?'

Her eyes scanned the page. The headline seemed to leap out at her. 'Fears Held For Safety. Gone to Ground?' Beneath it there was an article about Sam Darcy, 'recovering now from a suicide attempt', who held grave fears for the safety of Alexa Severn. She had, the newspaper informed its readers, been met at Auckland Airport, but no one had seen her after that. Her father refused to speak to the Press but it was reliably known that she had not arrived at his station.

Alexa bit her lip but said scornfully, 'Now I know it's the silly season. That's just a rehash.'

'Finish it,' he said implacably.

Angry, yet shrinking, she finished the paragraph, her expression pale with distaste as she read that Sam was worried about her eventual safety, he loved her and he wanted her to come back to him.

'Oh, dear lord,' she whispered.

He laughed harshly. 'Amazing, isn't it? However good you are in bed, you're not worth that sort of degradation.'

Oh, that hurt. But she thrust the pain away. 'I can't believe that he actually said that.' Her voice was dull as she tried to reconcile her dignified mentor with the sensational phraseology. 'It's just not Sam. He wouldn't say that sort of thing. He's too—too restrained.'

He shrugged and took the newspaper from her. 'He did say it,' he said indifferently. 'Here it is.'

'I'd have thought that you, of all people, should know how accurate newspapers needn't be.'

'Gossip columnists certainly, but this is not gossip. It's news, collated in London, sent here by Reuter. And the man is in love with you. Naturally he wants you back in his bed.'

She gave up. Very composedly, because she was keeping such a tight rein on herself, she said, 'I have never slept with Sam. Ever. I think it would be better if I went back home.'

'No.' The word was delivered with curt authority. 'You'll be better off here where I can keep an eye on you.'

She watched him walk out of the room, realising that he didn't believe a word that she had said.

'Oh, Sam,' she whispered, 'why did you do that?'

For the rest of the afternoon she was left with her own thoughts and a pile of glossy magazines. Her thoughts were totally depressing, so she read the magazines.

Interesting as they were, they began to pall after a short while. She leaned her glossy black head against the back of the chair and wondered where she would be today if she had followed her own inclinations and not allowed herself to be seduced by the blandishments of her mother. No, that was unfair. It was her own need to be praised by her mother that had led to all this.

If she had kept on the track she had laid out for herself she would be in some university somewhere, no doubt, restless and worried because she was teaching when all she wanted to do was follow her bent and explore some of the more esoteric sideways of mathematics.

Her lashes fluttered; she sank into an uncomfortable sleep and woke to a dry mouth and the memory of pages of equations dancing before her in her dreams. She found the sheet of paper she had been working on before lunch and began to write the symbols down, her brow furrowed as the pen slipped across the paper. Once she gave a groan of despair and crossed out half a page, but mostly it was a logical progression.

When someone came into the room she ignored them, muttering slightly in her haste to get the ideas down before they escaped. It felt—good; she was alive again after a long sleep.

At last her brain signalled tiredness and she put the pen down with a long sigh, flexing tired fingers, the symbols dancing in front of her eyes.

Leon's voice came as a distinct shock to her. 'What the hell have you been doing?'

She shrugged, then decided to tell him. 'Have you heard of the Elliott wave theory?'

In an arrested voice he said, 'Yes.'

It was her turn to be surprised. He gave her a glance of sardonic amusement. 'I deal to a certain extent with futures. Anything that might help me get a handle on the market is bound to be of interest.'

'It interests me, too. Also Fibonacci's numbers, on which Elliott based his theories. And Kondratieff's cycle of upswing, crisis and depression in the world economy.'

'Kondratieff was sent to Siberia for his beliefs.'

She bit her lip, because the amusement in his voice was open and demeaning. 'Fortunately we live in less repressive times,' she said quietly.

'All right,' he returned, 'so I understand your interest, although it was no wonder the market panicked when it became known that you were working according to a highly controversial and speculative set of theories.'

'The market panicked when I became stigmatised as Sam's mistress,' she retorted acidly. 'Until then, every-thing I'd done worked out well. If you'd like to look a little beyond that enormous set of prejudices and con-clusions you think are your opinions, and actually check the facts, you'd see that I didn't lose anyone any money. In fact, I made a lot.'

He didn't accept the challenge, merely lifted his brows. A long finger touched the sheets of paper in her lap. 'What is this?'

'I have toyed with the idea of finding some sort of mathematical correlation between the various rhythms, circadian, the sunspot cycle, and longer, less obvious rhythms.'

His brows contracted. He asked shortly, 'As in astrology?'

'Possibly.'

He leaned down to take a closer look at the sheet of paper in her lap. 'That doesn't look like astrological signs.'

'They're not. They're mathematical symbols.' And as his brows lifted she said gently, 'I have a doctorate. I know what I'm talking about.'

This did astonish him. He said harshly, 'I thought you graduated in management.'

'I did, after I got my doctorate. It is possible to follow two courses.'

'I see.' He didn't, but obviously he wasn't going to follow this up. Instead, he said coolly, 'What made you go into sordid commerce?'

'I wanted to please my mother.' A self-mocking, hard little smile straightened her mouth. 'Ironic, wasn't it. She didn't want an ivory tower mathematician. "So boring, darling, and no one will want to marry you if you spend all your time fiddling about with set squares and things. Men hate clever women, and let's face it, dear, you're not getting any younger."' Her mimicry of her mother's accent was perfect. 'So I went off to take the commercial world by storm. It had just become fashionable to become a whizzkid in the City.'

'Poor little misunderstood mathematician,' he taunted.

Why expose herself when he refused to believe her? It would be a lot easier if she stopped giving him opportunities to cut her down. So she lifted her shoulders in a shrug and said equably, 'Ah, well, it was fun while it lasted.'

'A very sensible attitude,' he said, straightening up. 'Cut your losses and look around for someone else to rely on.'

'No. From now on I rely only on myself.'

He laughed at that, and touched the curl of her ear, the smooth high sweep of her cheekbones with a lazy, caressing finger. 'No, don't do that. Think of the men you'll be depriving of the pleasure of losing themselves in that delectable long body, men blind and deaf with passion because you have made them so, men who would kill to own you...'

'Men like you?'

The smoky heat of his tones was wiped away, replaced by a hard confident amusement. 'No. Not me. I'm different. I know you for what you are, Alexa, a beautiful, clever bitch with a strange set of morals and a twisted outlook, but a beautiful, sensual body. When I take you it will be me who is in charge, not you. I won't surrender my integrity for any woman.'

He bent and kissed her mouth, hard and hot and demanding, his fingers tangling in the warm black locks at the nape of her neck to pull her head back, exposing the sunkissed length of her throat to a hungry exploration.

She flinched, and the stinging pressure gentled. His breath came hot across her skin as he whispered something against the throbbing pulse at the base of her throat. A tiny sound sighed through her lips and he straightened up, eyes that were almost black noting with a cold detachment the kiss-stung red of her mouth against the pallor of her face.

'Don't forget that,' he said. 'I make the rules here.'

She watched him go through the door with bleak anger. When he had disappeared her hand crept slowly up to her lips and touched their satiny fullness. On a half-sob she looked down at the paper in her lap, waiting for the moisture in her gaze to disappear so that she could see the figures and symbols again.

Outside the wind beat implacably at the island.

She didn't see him again until just before dinner, when she had changed into clothes a little more formal than the skirt and blouse she was wearing. Dressed in a silk shirt and trousers of a warm amber shade, she came out of her room and down the stairs.

As she drew near the open door to the study she heard voices, and although she tried to get past quickly, the traditional fate of the eavesdropper befell her.

'...I must say either she or you is a fast worker. Be careful—the lady's caused a lot of damage to her other protector.' Chris, striving for worldliness.

'I'm not as easily impressed as Sam Darcy.' Leon's voice was extremely dry.

'Poor old Darcy. Mind you,' he said with a touch of lustfulness, 'I can see what she has. I'd have thought old Darcy a little too proper to have indulged in a sizzling affair, but you just never know, do you? I certainly didn't expect to find her here! I must say, she doesn't look the sort to throw the stock market into a panic!'

'There is a type?' Leon's voice was exceptionally dry.

'Well, I'd have thought she'd be harder...tougher-looking. She strikes me as being almost subdued. Most women who sleep their way through life get that shiny look, all slick and sophisticated and ready for anything. She behaves a bit like a rather severe older sister.'

Leon said idly, 'You like her, I gather.'

'Well—yes. Yes. I gather you don't.'

'Liking is not exactly how I would describe my feelings towards the lady. Like you, I found her to be a surprise.'

Chris laughed but refused to accept the reply. 'So, what do you think? Was it just a coincidence that she turned up here, or is she on the lookout for another "sugar daddy"?'

'Your terminology is out of date,' Leon said absently, while Alexa seethed.

'Stop avoiding the issue.'

'I think that she came here to meet me, yes. As for the other, I can only admire a woman who is so dedicated to her own advancement.'

The unsparing note in his voice brought a boyish whistle from his brother and a cold premonition to the unwilling eavesdropper.

'So—keep off?' Chris sounded a little disappointed.

Leon said amusedly, 'Oh-ho, had you designs on the lady?'

'Oh, well, I thought she might want a little light relief. Poor old Darcy must have been heavy weather for her. However, if you've got your eye on her, I'll willingly retire. Women never see me when you're around.'

'You underestimate yourself. This one, however, I want.'

Just that blatant declaration, delivered with casual arrogance. Alexa found herself rigid with rage, but beneath that was a fear that was the stronger for being firmly repressed. Stiffly, no longer caring about whether they heard her or not, she strode past the door and on to the sitting-room. They arrived five minutes later, smoothly courteous. Their manners, she thought sourly, were superb.

Dinner was superb too, a chicken and melon salad to begin, with an interesting mayonnaise that seemed to be made mostly of finely ground nuts, followed by *hapuku*, a deep sea groper from far out in the bay, served in a casserole with capsicums and chickpeas and tomatoes. And after that the housekeeper brought in plums poached in port and decorated with pink praline and a swirl of cream. A delicious Sauvignon Blanc from

Marlborough in the South Island complemented the food.

Yet in spite of the inspired cooking, Alexa found it difficult to get a mouthful past the lump in her throat. The two men made polite conversation. It was obvious that Chris didn't realise that his casual, insulting words had been overheard, but it was impossible for her to tell whether Leon knew or not. His expression was totally impassive with nothing more to lighten their depths than a glitter of sensual appreciation whenever his eyes met hers.

Outside the wind was still tearing at the house, its force not apparently dampened by the heavy rain that accompanied it. There was nothing more to be done. Now, as Chris observed when they went back to the sitting-room, it was just a matter of waiting.

'At least,' he said cheerfully when Alexa rose to go to bed an hour or so of polite, amusing conversation later, 'we're not likely to have power cuts. Having our own generator puts us at an advantage.'

'Unless something ominous happens to the generator.'

He grinned. 'No. It wouldn't dare. It belongs to Leon Venetos!'

His brother laughed and so, after a moment, did Alexa. There was enough of the cheeky small boy left in Chris to make him hard to resist.

Alexa said goodnight, smiling rather austerely at Chris's enthusiastic farewell. Not that his attitude to women was all his fault; with an older brother like Leon, how could he be expected to see women as anything more than a temporary convenience?

Some time during the night she woke to a fury of noise.

The wind howled around the house, not in the quick bursts of the evening, but with a steadily rising tone that spoke of force unimaginable, a battering, ferocious tantrum of nature directed with indifference at anything in its path.

Alexa shivered, remembering that out at sea yachts were racing from Australia to Auckland. Had they been close enough to the coast of New Zealand to be in danger? She couldn't remember what she had seen or heard on the news the evening before; she had been so angry with Leon that the usual dose of gloom and misery had passed right over her.

Rain came roaring over the hills and crashed into the house, then over and on past it, out across the water to the mainland. There was a moment's ominous stillness before the wind hammered again into the trees and the house, driving more rain before it in a solid sheet. Bolt upright in bed, Alexa watched with alarm as the curtains billowed into the room and were suddenly sucked out through the french doors. She sprang from the bed and ran across to pull them inside, wrestling with the reluctant doors until she got them locked, then wondered if perhaps she should pull the shutters across too. After all, it would have been weather like this that they had been made to deal with.

But the wind was coming from the east, not from the west, and for the time being the homestead was sheltered by the bulk of the island. Uneasily, she stood watching the wild confusion of tossing palm fronds against a dark and heaving sea, before turning back to the bed.

She was sitting on the edge, her open eyes straining through the darkness, when something pulled her head around to the door. It was so dark that she shouldn't have been able to see anything at all, yet there was a flicker in the darkness and she knew that Leon had come in. He must have been half-way across the room when she sensed his presence because he was in front of her almost immediately.

Against the cacophony of sound outside his voice was deep and reassuring as he asked, 'Are you all right?'

'Yes.'

She jumped as his hand touched her shoulder. 'Then why are you so tense?'

'I keep listening for crashes.'

In a smooth movement he lowered himself on to the bed and scooped her up into his arms, holding her against his big warm body as he stretched back against the pillows. She made no sound, but the uproar of the cyclone faded against the rapid beating of her heart. Efficiently, as though he did this every night, he pulled the sheet up over them both and said pleasantly, 'Try to get some sleep.'

For the first time in her life she felt the warm rough hardness of a man's chest beneath her cheek. He smelt of male, very slightly salty with a faint hint of musk; evocative, extremely erotic, pulling at nerves she didn't know she possessed, summoning ancient longings from a pagan primitive past.

Her mind told her coolly and rationally that this summons, this powerful urge to lose herself in the delights of the flesh, this blind hunger, was natural and normal. All life was programmed to perpetuate the species, and sexuality came wrapped up in as many exciting little packages as there were organisms. She was of an age to bear children, and he was a virile man; naturally, they were impelled together. And the spice of danger that the storm represented was an added relish to that basic urge.

But she had not known how powerfully intoxicating was the heat from a man's body, or the smooth hardness

of masculine muscles beneath fine-grained skin, how incredibly seductive the illusion of security that a woman
gained from being locked in his embrace.

A pretty little package, indeed! It was more like an
explosion, as much a storm as the one that blustered
outside.

He was just being kind, she reminded herself. He could
be kind; it was an odd characteristic in a man as arrogantly masculine as Leon, but she had always recognised
that basic compassion, as well as his integrity.

He moved, pulling her with him so that she lay half
over him, her head tucked into the hollow of his
shoulder. 'I'm too heavy,' she thought, panic-stricken,
but she didn't move. His hand came up and began to
smooth the heavy locks of her hair. She was profoundly
grateful for her long nightgown because it provided some
sort of barrier between them. She didn't think he had
much on; he certainly wore no jacket.

She certainly wasn't going to try to find out whether
he had pants on.

His hand moved slowly over her hair, lifting the damp
little tendrils at her brow, curling them over his fore-
finger, threading through the heavy mass at the nape of
her neck. His fingers stroked slowly, evenly, across the
sensitive hollows at her temples, lifting the weight of silk
away from her skin, letting it sift down again.

If it was meant to be soothing he was missing the point.
Alexa had to concentrate on keeping her breathing slow
and even; in, out, in, out; while the ferocity of the storm
seemed strangely muted against the noise of her
heartbeats.

Little tendrils of fire were snaking through her body.
With a desperate effort she thought they were probably
following the hidden pathways all the way from her brain

to every nerve-end, sparking, sending erotic, stinging little messages to each receptor until she was sizzling with sensation.

It was difficult to think logically when her heart was thundering in her breast so loudly that the wind was a mere sigh above it. But she tried. Whatever else had happened to her in the past, her brain had never let her down. However, although it was functioning now, it was certainly not behaving normally. Gone was the logic, and the rational thought processes, lost in a web of sensuality, so that her mind acted only as a receiving station for feelings and emotions she had never before experienced.

She felt liquid and waiting, yearning for something...

Leon lowered his head and asked conversationally, 'Why are you trembling?'

'I—I don't know.' A brilliant answer, she thought miserably.

'The wind is not likely to get any worse.'

'No.'

'Is it the storm?'

Shut up, her brain urged. Aloud she said slowly, 'I—yes.'

Of course it wasn't, but how could she tell him that? He'd laugh like the predator he was and lose no time in taking advantage of her weakness.

Even above the sound of the wind she could discern the amusement in his voice when he replied smoothly, 'Really? You strike me as being too sensible a woman to be afraid of a storm. The worst that can happen is that the roof could come off, but the homestead was repaired and renovated only two years ago, so it's not likely. If the creeks flood we're well above flood-level. And if the wind pounds in from the west, as it's likely to do once the eye has passed over us, it will be at low tide, so the garden should be quite safe. I have never heard of tidal surges from a cyclone this far south, although I suppose it could happen. But we're at least thirty feet above sea-level, so it would have to be a big one to do us any harm.'

He paused as though inviting comment, but when she made no reply he resumed smoothly, 'But perhaps it's not the storm that is making your heart beat double time, Alexa. Not the storm outside, anyway.'

The smell of danger filled her nostrils. In sheer panic she jerked away, trying to fling herself off the bed, but his arms closed smoothly, fiercely around her.

'Well, Alexa?' The words were a taunt, a sneer, yet through the sardonic tone she caught echoes of her own condition, a need that was too big for all the other emotions, the distrust and the contempt and the control.

Like her, Leon was in thrall to a desire he couldn't handle except by repressing it. The knowledge gave her the freedom to accept what she was doing. With a twist of her body she turned towards him. She muttered, 'Damn you!' and cut off his answer by pressing her open mouth over his.

There was a moment's instinctive rejection. Leon was accustomed to making the advances—or repelling them; whatever, he was always the one who controlled. This time it would be different. He would learn that making love need not be an exercise in restraint and control.

But even as her mind formed the thought it was gone, swamped by a multitude of sensations encouraged by his response to her kiss.

She expected him to be a fierce lover, and he was, but his strength was tempered by an instinctive understanding of the nuances of lovemaking. As his mouth gentled over hers she realised that her virginal fears of ardour close to rape were not going to be realised. He showed his experience by the skilful way he touched her, the sinful, sensual slide of his hands across her skin as he removed the nightdress from her shaking body.

'I'm not going to hurt you,' he whispered against her throat.

'I—I know.' The words chattered out and, in case he should wonder why the intimacy of their positions caused such a reaction in her, she put her mouth to his shoulder and kissed a smooth bulge of muscle, fascinated to realise that his breath stopped in his throat, and the lean body stiffened.

His response, unguarded and involuntary, emboldened her. With the tip of her tongue she traced a line along his collarbone. He tasted of salt and some primeval masculine flavour that she had never noticed before, but that she recognised.

Aroused male. Somewhere her brain found the time to wonder if she too had her own particular scent, so faint that only a man who held her could recognise it, and know by it that she was receptive.

Her hand spread out over his chest, fingertips sensitive and seeking, learning him by touch. The wide expanse, the soft curls of hair scrolled in an eminently satisfying pattern, the small tight nipples. She hesitated, and he groaned something against her throat. Ducking, she touched one with her tongue, and felt it stiffen and grow hard. At the same time her own peaked with an urgent inrush of sensation. She gasped, and in a movement that took her by surprise he rolled her on to her back and pushed up her breast with one hand, the other tangled in the hair at the back of her head.

She didn't know what to expect. How could she have known that he would kiss her throat, and the long lovely line from there to her breast; how could she have known that his hand would curve so lovingly around her fullness, holding still until that searching mouth could find the sensitive nipple? Her breath tore into her lungs.

She heard him laugh, a low, triumphant sound, and then his mouth closed over it and for the first time in her life she knew what it felt like to have a man suckle her.

Her body arched in a spasm of sensation. Needles of fire stung and sprang through her body, sparking every cell into life, until she felt that she had to be luminous, her tissues glowing fiercely in the darkened room while his mouth revealed to her everything she had missed in her life until that moment.

'Gently,' he breathed, turning his head against the soft mound so that she felt the burning heat of his face. 'Alexa—touch me.'

Her hand was shaking, trembling, the fingers desperate yet afraid as they reached out for him. She felt the great heat of his body, the intense restraint that locked his muscles, the unknown yet deeply familiar masculine angles and planes, and all the while he too was exploring her as though she was some beloved country, only his, his only to take and conquer and love and live with...

She said nothing, beyond an occasional whimper that broke from her throat when she was threatened with swamping by the sensuality she had never suspected lurked latent within her. He too was silent, but they communicated in a way known only to lovers, hand and mouth and tiny imperceptible movements of muscle and skin. She did not have to tell him that his mouth on the sensitive skin of her stomach was tormenting; he knew. Just as she knew that when she explored the tight masculine curve of his buttocks and the long sweep of muscle from thigh to hip, it made him forget the storm that raged outside for the just as elemental one that was drawing them, inexorably, closer to the greatest mystery of all.

When it came there was a little pain, but it was over immediately, and she was lost in the wonder of it as he made himself master of her body with one powerful thrust, imprinting on her the strength and force of his masculinity, and she accepted it, took him within her with joy and a fierce possessive delight.

It was like being consumed by fire, flames licking over her and through her and inside her, yet there was something of the earth and the wind and the wild tumult outside in their joining, so that at times she thought she would die of the heat, and at others she felt helpless before the force of his possession. He made himself free of her body with a savage desire that should have terrified her virgin heart, yet there was tenderness there in his arms, imprisoned by his desire, and grace, and something else, a consideration she had never expected.

For a few minutes, for aeons of time, the intellect she had grown to think her only asset, her only reason for pride, was obliterated, swept away and denied by this other force. Wooed by his ardour, lost in the sensual world of their making, Alexa understood what it was to be a woman fulfilled. And with the understanding came a glory, a delight in her body and his, a comprehension of the physical bonds that true union can weave about the mind and the heart and the body.

Dazedly, out of control as her body thrust and met his, taken over by the tides of need, she found herself sobbing, borne up and up towards a destination that seemed at once so close and so distant, within her yet dependent on the thrusts of the powerful body above and within hers.

His name broke from her lips and the bubble of sensation shattered, flowered into fragments, took her with him in an ecstasy so intense that she thought she must faint with the intolerable pleasure. Yet it was an almost greater pleasure to hear the groan that resounded through him, and feel his taut ecstasy as he attained his climax.

She had read enough about sex, listened to women and a few men talk about it. She understood enough of the technical aspects to know that this rapture was rare for a virgin. Yet no one had ever told her that afterwards there was a kind of ecstasy in lying pressed beneath an exhausted man, his head in the angle of her shoulder, his chest lifting and falling as he took great shuddering breaths.

No one had ever said that it was sweet to stroke his hair back from his face and feel it damp across her fingers, to run her hands over skin slick and hot; it was delicious to feel languor creep stealthily through bones and limbs that ached with unaccustomed exercise. Alexa had never felt so safe, even though the wind outside was building to some sort of devil's crescendo and the roof was creaking and moaning as though mortally wounded.

At last Leon's breath began to sound normal. He lifted his head and asked with a chilling lack of expression, 'How is it that Sam Darcy's mistress is so hungry for it that she makes all the running?'

All of Alexa's new-found contentment vanished. Her body shrank away, and he said bitingly, 'It's too late for that now. Was he impotent, Alexa? Did he have other methods of achieving release?'

She felt as though a cover had been ripped off something beautiful to reveal only foulness beneath. All that had happened, her joyous surrender to the physical side of her nature, was shown for the sordid opportunism that it was. To be dashed from delight and satiety to contempt was shattering. She could only deal with it by her usual method of hiding away, by pulling a cloak over her tender feelings and refusing to admit to them.

After all, she thought bitterly, it had worked for her in the past. It was going to have to do the job now. Later, perhaps, when she was safely alone, she would deal with the disillusion.

Her voice was cold, toneless. 'I told you, I was never Sam's mistress.'

'I find that hard to believe. Presumably you gave him reason to think that his avowal of love to the media would be reciprocated.'

She bit her lip. 'I don't know why he did that. He must be temporarily unhinged by the exhibition his wife is making of herself. I didn't lie to you.'

He rolled away from her and lay on his back in the big bed, staring up at the ceiling. Alexa felt ice chill her bones, creep slowly, sluggishly through her body. She had thought—oh, her naïveté was stupendous! Somehow she had thought that such a perfect lovemaking would engender trust as close as the physical trust that had bound them together.

But it had solved nothing. To Leon she was just another woman in his bed.

In a voice muffled with exhaustion she said, 'Can you go back to your room now?'

'You're so cold,' he said savagely. 'Ice-cold, so cold you burn my fingers when I touch you. Ten minutes ago you were sobbing in my arms, sheathing me in heat, sweet and tight, silken legs holding me in place, and now you banish me as if it never happened. What does it take for you to lose control, damn it?'

Her bitter laughter made him freeze, but after a shocked second he said angrily, 'Oh, not physically. You are all that a man could ask for, wild and sweet and pagan. But that's not enough. Your brain, that cool detached part of you that you shelter in, watched everything, didn't it? Classifying and ticketing and arranging, slotting this whole experience into some sort of category to be retrieved if necessary at some future date!'

Alexa was afraid of the dark force of his anger, bewildered by his reaction to her calmness. 'Why should you want me to lose control?' she asked steadily.

'Perhaps because it would show that you are human, not just a beautiful robot programmed to make love.'

The sheer cruelty of the words made her flinch. He felt it, because he said something beneath his breath and laughed mirthlessly. 'Why did that hurt? What are you?'

'I told you that I—that Sam and I were not lovers. It's not my fault that you choose to believe lies.'

'Then why the hell did he flip his lid so crazily about you?'

'I—he thought—thinks—he's in love with me. He—we've worked together for all this time and we got on so well until a few months ago. And then——' she paused, wondering if she was mad to try to convince him. 'He changed. I didn't know how to cope with it. I thought if I ignored it he might get over it. Because I'm sure he's not in love with me. I honestly never thought of him as anything other than a friend and a mentor.'

Her breath lodged in her throat as she waited for his answer. He ran a possessive hand down the length of her body, pausing when it came to her breasts. 'You are so beautiful,' he said in a shaken voice. 'So wildly, wantonly beautiful, and it doesn't mean anything to you, does it? Have you ever been in love, Alexa?'

She was aching with disillusion. Yet the truth came to her lips. 'I've always steered clear of loving anyone. It doesn't seem to work for my family. My mother still loves my father, and my father is still in love with my mother. His wife loves him obsessively, and makes his life a misery with her jealousy. The Severns don't seem to do love very well.'

'So you shut yourself away.'

Had she? Perhaps not consciously, but she could see now that she had been careful to avoid emotional entanglements. Fastidity and sheer hard work had all played a part in her continuing virginity, but he was right, the main reason for it had been fear.

'So what do you do now?' he asked, when her silence had stretched to an uncomfortable length.

She wanted to ask him if he believed her, but she was proud, too proud to demand a reply. Perhaps he needed to think things over.

She said quietly, 'I won't be a nuisance.'

He said something in Italian, something she was rather glad she didn't understand, and went on in a low, fierce undertone, 'You are a nuisance. You're an entanglement I could well do without. You terrify me and fascinate me and infuriate me, and now that I know that beneath that frigid exterior there's a woman of fire, I'm afraid that I'm going to want to take you again and again, until I've quenched the fire you lit in me with the ice you wrap your emotions in.'

Sheer panic held her rigid. 'No!' But even as the word burst through her lips he drew her closer, his hands cruel on her skin, and she surrendered after only the shortest of struggles, her body so attuned to the needs and desires of his that she could not fight it.

This time it was a pagan primitive ritual; Leon behaved as though he wanted to stamp the authority of his possession on to her, make her no more than a slave to the passion that burned them both. It should have been degrading but, because he too was unable to resist, because every surrender forced from her was matched by a responding surrender from him, there was no degradation. They came together as equals in a conflagration that made her moan as the violent, erotic waves of sensation took her under.

Afterwards, when sanity returned, she tried to pull away, but he said, 'No, stay there,' in a slurred voice, and tucked her against him, spoon fashion. Exhausted, she slid into sleep with his hand curved possessively over her breast, while outside the wind howled and pounded and attacked.

When she awoke it was morning, a dull grey light seeping in through the windows, and someone was hammering at the door, calling Leon's name.

CHAPTER SIX

ALEXA was still muttering and opening her eyes when the door was opened and Chris hurtled impetuously in. Leon hauled Alexa against him, pressing her face to his chest. His voice cracked out, sharp as a whip. 'Get out!'

'Damn it, Leon, I don't care who you've got in bed with you! There's a yacht out off Honeymoon Bay and it's not going to make it. It looks as though it's going to break up! I swear they've got no steerage; they're headed straight on to the reef!'

Alexa said, 'Oh, dear heaven,' and pushed away. Sharply she demanded, 'Exactly where are they?'

'In a line from the headland between us and the highest hill on the mainland.'

White to the lips she looked at Leon. 'At least three yachts were wrecked there while we lived here. There's no passage through that reef.'

He was out of the bed, not trying to hide his nakedness. 'I know. Chris, get on the radio to Search and Rescue—no, first tell Raewyn to get all of the men out of bed.'

Chris disappeared and Alexa looked at Leon as he hauled on the dressing gown he had discarded the night before. 'What are you going to do?'

'I don't know, but if they've got no steerage they're going to have to be taken off that yacht.' He paused long enough to say, 'Don't panic. Chris is inclined to exaggerate.'

But twenty minutes later, on top of the hill above the bay, he was forced to admit that this time there had been no exaggeration. The yacht was definitely in severe trouble.

Alexa had insisted on going with them. Although Leon had pushed her against the sheltered side of the Range Rover, she was gasping as the wind did its best to blow the breath out of her body. Through narrowed eyes she discovered the small keel tossing in the grey waste of the sea, and found that she was whispering scraps of prayers under her breath. Beside her most of the men from the island watched through binoculars.

One said, 'There's only one man aboard by the looks of it.'

'He's never going to make it into shelter!' Chris was looking at Leon as though he alone was capable of rescuing it.

Alexa felt a sudden pang of fear. Surely—surely Leon wouldn't try to go out in that maelstrom? The channel was exposed to the full force of the storm, and the waves that were roaring in to smash themselves on to the coast were enormous, the spray whipped from them into screaming spindrift that formed a thick murk, so that the tiny yacht was often lost to view. More often, it was hidden by one of the monster waves so that all that could be discerned was the frail top of its mast.

Sean said angrily, 'He must be a rank amateur. He should be carrying more sail than that stupid scrap of jib. It's no wonder he's got no steerage.'

Someone else said, 'Could have blown it out.'

'Well, if something's not done about it,' Sean said in a pugnacious voice, 'he's going to end smashed up on the reef and I doubt very much whether he'll live through those waves.'

Every eye turned to the savage fury of water over the long reef that stretched out towards the mainland. Even to a person with no knowledge of the sea and boats it was plain that the yacht had no hope of clawing free of danger.

Leon was frowning as he watched through field-glasses the tiny scrap of man's ingenuity, almost completely overwhelmed by the effortless malice of nature. With a sinking heart Alexa realised that he was making a decision, and even as her heart stopped she knew what that decision was going to be.

Looking at Sean, he asked, 'Can you see any prospect of them getting across the reef?'

He didn't need Sean's oath, or the quick reply. 'No. Not a hope.'

'Then we'll have to take the cabin cruiser out and tow him back in.'

Alexa didn't recognise her own voice as she asked, 'And if you can't?'

Without looking at her he said casually, 'We'll take him off. He's not going to live much longer. That's no blue-water keel, it's a little day-sailor, and it's just not built to last in this sort of weather.'

A wild gust emphasised his words even as it tore them away. Alexa looked from Leon's face, almost impassive as he watched the pathetic little scrap of sail in the wilderness of the waters, and saw that there was no way she could stop him from going out and doing what he could. He didn't look as though he would enjoy it, merely totally confident that, if it had to be done, he would do it.

It was in that moment that she realised that she loved him.

Hopelessly, irrevocably, for the rest of her life. For eternity. So much that it was like a coming home and the discovery of a new world. It should have been a joyous understanding, but her heart wept, and it was all she could do to climb back into the Range Rover and go down the hill.

Raewyn was appalled when she heard what they planned to do, but she said, 'If anyone can do it, Leon will. And Sean is almost as competent as he is.'

But this knowledge did not help Alexa when she watched the big cabin cruiser head into the tossing, threatening sea. A superstition of her mother's came into her head. Never watch anyone go right out of sight, she said. If you do they might never come back.

She turned away, catching Chris's belligerent gaze with an attempt at a smile. He said curtly. 'I should be with him instead of Sean.'

'He knows the bay like the back of his hand,' she said placatingly, understanding the hurt to his pride.

'Yes, well, there was no need for Leon to be so blasted rude when I suggested it!'

Alexa laughed, and after a moment he gave a wry grin. 'I suppose you're right, when has he not behaved as though he's lord of the universe? Are you coming up on to the hill to watch?'

She couldn't bear to watch; she couldn't bear not to. 'Yes.'

Everyone else was back up there, in spite of wind strong enough to rock the Range Rover, and the sudden ferocious showers of rain. No one said much. They watched in silence as the big cruiser battled out through the waves. When it got out of the lee of the island and turned to take the waves on the bow Alexa gave a soundless gasp, for even without glasses it was obvious that the sea was a killer. She dragged her eyes away from the scene below to look at the horizon. There was no consolation there. A wildly scudding sky promised only further and worse weather.

The little yacht was now well within the line of the reef, heading slowly but inexorably towards a doom that was certain unless *The Dove* got to it before it reached the greedy rocks.

One of the men was telling another without binoculars what was happening as the bigger craft at last arrived on the scene, perilously close to where the water began to break in a seething fury above the reef.

'Can't quite see—ah, yes, they've got the line across.' He watched fixedly, then said, 'Chap on the keel doesn't seem to know—yeah, he's made fast now. They're turning—yeah, looks like they've done it. Hell, Leon's bloody brilliant at the helm. Looks as though they're going to make it. If the bloke in the keel knows how to manage it under tow.'

Alexa tasted blood in her mouth and looked around hurriedly, conscious of a stinging in her eyes that had nothing to do with the wind. Everyone was smiling, although they all knew that there was still danger until the linked craft made it around the end of the reef and into its shelter. Even there the waves were ferocious, until compared to the seething fury beyond.

They watched until the cruiser reached those comparatively calm waters, and then everyone smiled, and Raewyn said briskly, 'I'd better get down and make something hot for them.' She looked at Alexa. 'And you are to come down with us. No, the boss said so. No hanging about in the weather.'

So Alexa meekly rode back down the hill and occupied herself by making up a bed in one of the bedrooms for the shipwrecked sailor. Raewyn protested, but Alexa managed to convince her to stay in the kitchen and prepare an enormous breakfast.

When at length the cruiser towed its burden into the bay she was watching from the sun-room, the housekeeper beside her. The little yacht anchored in the lee of the cruiser and, to the astonishment of both women, there were now two adults on deck.

'I wonder where...' Raewyn stopped, then, 'Alexa, can you see? It looks to me as though they're handing up children!'

'Two.' Alexa was astounded. 'Those poor parents!'

Five minutes later Leon and Sean came in, both carrying a small child, followed closely by a man and a woman whose faces revealed only too clearly the ordeal they had endured.

Alexa's nose wrinkled at the odour. Someone had been sick. Stepping forward, she held out her arms for the biggest child, a girl of about three. 'Hello,' she said cheerfully. 'Would like a nice warm bath and some dry clothes?'

The child looked at her mother, received a short nod, and smiled shyly at her before nodding.

'I'll take her,' she said to Leon, who looked down at her knee; her eyes flicked beyond him and she added in an urgent undertone, 'Look out for the mother.'

He relinquished the child only just in time. As Alexa bore her out of the room he and the father grabbed the fainting woman. Hastily, she went through the door so that the child in her arms couldn't see what was happening. Sean followed her with the smaller of the children, a little boy. When they had got to the bathroom he looked around the luxurious room and as he set the boy down said explosively, 'She's pregnant! She was down below with the children, that's why we couldn't see them.'

The children looked at him, an identical expression of fear on both little faces, and he said apologetically, 'Sorry. I—do you need any help?'

Alexa had never bathed children before, but it was unlikely that Sean would be able to give her any hints, so she said serenely, 'No, off you go. We'll be fine, won't we kids?'

They looked somewhat taken aback at being directly addressed, but smiled shyly in response, and with a relieved grin Sean took himself off, after promising to get some clothes for them from one of the shepherds' wives, who had children of roughly the same size.

'What are your names?' Alexa asked, removing the little life-jackets with a practised hand. 'Mine's Alexa. Can you say that?'

The small girl had a go at it and produced Lexy, while her brother smiled around the thumb in his mouth and refused to try.

A noise in the passage outside took her across to the half-open door. Leon was coming up the last few stairs with the children's mother in his arms. She was still unconscious. Quietly Alexa closed the door and turned to survey the two small faces watching her so warily.

'I'll put some water in the bath,' she suited her actions to the words, 'and then we'll take off these clothes, shall we, and you can get all nice and clean and warm again?'

'My name's Jodie.'

The little boy said, 'Dodie,' around his thumb, watching with respect as the water ran into the big green bath.

'That's pretty,' Alexa said. 'Can you get undressed yourself?'

Jodie nodded and confided, 'But not the buttons. Mummy does those. Paul can't get himself undressed at all.'

'Never mind, I'll undress Paul and undo your buttons.'

They had a pleasant bath, Jodie revealing herself to be a chatterbox, and Paul forgot his thumb for long enough to laugh out loud and splash.

They were reduced to silence by the arrival of the shepherd's wife, rosy-cheeked and smelling of rain, who bore a box of clothes and another of toys. She didn't stay and, when she had gone, Jodie said, 'The boat went round and round and up and down and Daddy wouldn't come down the stairs. Mummy was sick. Paul and me was scared.'

'I suppose you were.' Alexa whisked her out of the bath and handed her a huge towel, then coaxed Paul forth. 'Anyone would have been frightened. But it's all right now.'

Jodie made a pretty good job of drying herself, and of dressing in the overalls and T-shirt that fitted her. She giggled when Paul made it difficult for Alexa by wriggling and trying to get back into the bath, but after they were dressed and combed and sweet-smelling once more, she asked with a trembling mouth, 'Where's my mummy?'

'Let's go and see,' Alexa suggested.

Hand in hand they went down the flight of stairs, slowly because Paul insisted on checking out the view between every one of the banisters. At the bottom they met Leon, changed also, his hair sleek and wet from the shower, very tall, very male.

Assailed by memories of her new-found discovery, Alexa refused to meet his eyes as she asked, 'Jodie and Paul would like to see their parents. Is it possible?'

'Mummy,' Paul said firmly.

Leon nodded, his expression austere. He smiled at the children, and they, no more impervious to that blatant charm than Alexa had been, smiled back. 'Yes,' he said. 'She's in bed in the room opposite yours.'

So they went back up the stairs and along the hall, then knocked at the door. Raewyn opened it, her normally serene expression a little harried, and said, 'Oh, good, you're here. Mrs Fairleigh has been worrying about you two.'

The children let go of Alexa's hands and scampered across the room to the bed where their mother lay. She was, Alexa was perturbed to see, pale and obviously still very shaken by her ordeal. Even as she smiled her face set into unmistakable lines of pain.

Alexa looked at the housekeeper, who was frowning as she watched. Sliding a meaningful glance at Alexa she said, 'I think you'd better warn Leon that we might be going to have a new baby.'

'Oh, lord!' Alexa swallowed. 'How close is she to her due date?'

'A month,' Raewyn said, adding inconsequentially, 'She told me that they weren't worried about going away because she is always at least a fortnight overdue.'

Alexa watched as the children climbed eagerly up on to the bed, telling their mother together about the bath and their new clothes. Then she turned and went out to find Leon.

Outside the wind pulled with greedy fingers at the fabric of the house, searching for weaknesses, howling with frustration when none were revealed. The solid walls didn't even creak as a wooden house would have done, and the heavy old walls kept much of the noise muffled, although the roof beams groaned from time to time.

On the landing Alexa's eyes were caught by the view from the window. Outside in the garden the palms were tossing in agony, their fronds painting great swathes against a sky of fleeing, boiling clouds. Even as she watched one frond was torn off and flung across the garden into the sea. Unable to bear it, Alexa turned away.

Leon was in the office, his brows drawn together in a black frown as he looked at a sheet of paper. Chris was saying urgently, 'According to the latest forecast they simply don't know what it's going to do. It appears to have stopped, and might even retrace its tracks. Apparently the only thing you can be sure of with a cyclone is that it never does what it's expected to do. This one's just running true to form.'

Leon looked up. He surveyed Alexa as though he had never seen her before, then demanded curtly. 'What is it?'

Alexa told him, and he swore and said, 'That's all we need!'

His callousness would have shocked Alexa if she hadn't discerned the deep concern beneath it.

'I suppose there's no way we could get her across to the mainland?' Chris offered tentatively, only to fall silent as a particularly savage gust hurled itself at the windows.

'Not a hope.' Leon looked at Alexa. 'Do you know anything about childbirth?'

'Only that it hurts,' she said, adding hurriedly, because it sounded so flippant and she hadn't meant it to, 'Raewyn seems to have some idea of what to do.'

'She's had children.' For the first time Leon looked not in command of the situation. He thought for a few moments then said decisively, 'Alexa, you get upstairs and see what's happening. Chris, get on the radio and find a doctor. If we're going to have an emergency we might as well know how to deal with it.'

Upstairs Raewyn was talking softly to Mr Fairleigh, a thin man, clad in what were clearly Chris's clothes, who looked far too young to be the father of a family, while the two children cuddled up to their mother on the wide bed.

Raewyn broke off her conversation and said cheerfully, 'I think the children might want a meal, Miss Severn. Would you like to take them down to the morning-room? There's food on the table——'

'I'll take care of everything.' Alexa went across to the bed, and smiled at the children. Clearly tired, they had perked up at the mention of food. 'Come on,' she said, holding out her hand. 'We'll go down and you can tell me what you'd like to eat.'

'Toast.' Like everything Paul had said, it was delivered with determination.

Alexa chuckled and addressed their mother. 'No allergies?'

'No. They eat anything.' She kissed them both. 'You be good for...'

'Lexy,' Jodie told her.

Paul echoed it, and their mother smiled. 'Be good for Lexy, and after you've had something to eat, you can help her with the dishes.'

Raewyn said firmly, 'Mr Fairleigh, why don't you go and have something to eat too? You need it.'

He hesitated, but when his wife seconded the suggestion he nodded, kissed her and followed Alexa and the children down the stairs.

Once in the morning-room Alexa set him to supervising the children's meals while she made toast and coffee, and poached a couple of eggs in the huge, opulently convenient kitchen. When she came back into the room he said diffidently, 'You are being so kind——'

'Nonsense,' she said briskly.

But he was determined. 'I honestly thought we'd had it. I was so angry with myself for putting us all in this situation, I felt sick with fear, and then your husband appeared out of the spray and the wind, and I thought we might have a chance. I can't describe how I felt.'

'He's not my husband,' she said calmly. 'Like you, I'm a guest here. However, I know how you felt. Leon has that air of total competence, hasn't he?' And because she did not want to go on discussing Leon, she continued without a pause, 'What exactly were you doing out there?'

'We've been moored in a little bay around the point for three days. It was lovely, so peaceful. We've both had really hectic times lately, and we just lazed around, swimming and having barbecues on the beach—I can't tell you how much we were enjoying ourselves. We honestly didn't think to listen to the weather forecast.

This came up out of the blue. Last night when it started to blow I realised that something pretty nasty was on the way, and we decided that as soon as it got light this morning we'd better get around the point into the shelter of the land, but although I reefed the mainsail right down it still blew out, and then I couldn't steer it properly with just the jib up.'

He drank some coffee. 'I could see the white water over the reefs. I thought we were goners.' His voice revealed the fear and the self-loathing. 'And then the launch appeared. Hell, I've never seen anything like it. They came out of the mist and the wind like Vikings. They manoeuvred so close, working the waves, not taking risks yet...'

He shivered and broke off, aware that the children, alerted by the tone of his voice, were watching him anxiously. 'And then we had a lumpy trip in,' he finished, smiling. 'And here we are, eating our breakfast.'

'And the nasty ol' wind is outside,' Jodie told him with satisfaction.

They looked around as Leon and Chris came into the room. In any other situation Alexa would have been amused at the fact that both father and children had the same wary, bemused expression. Not that she blamed them. When she looked at Leon she too felt a kind of awe. Unbidden memories of the night before brought a sudden heat to her skin. To hide the blush she went across to the sideboard to pour coffee for herself.

'Pour some for us, too, Alexa,' he said, before turning to his guest with a smile.

It was then that she saw Leon's public persona in action. From his attitude no one would have known that he was coping with a cyclone of possibly disastrous proportions and a woman who seemed about to deliver a premature baby. He was urbane, pleasant and perfectly friendly, so that in a short time the guests relaxed and the meal was eaten in an atmosphere of good humour.

Even Alexa, who thought she might die of embarrassment, found herself smiling and talking, slipping unostentatiously into the role of hostess and substitute mother, while outside the wind seemed to pick up speed and force.

Only once was it mentioned. Mr Fairleigh looked out after a particularly vicious gust and said almost to himself, 'I'm glad we're not out in that.'

Leon said nothing, and the man continued after a pause, 'This house isn't wooden, is it? There are none of the creaks and complaints wooden houses of this age usually indulge in during a storm.'

Leon said urbanely, 'Alexa knows all about the house. Her great-great-great-grandfather built it.'

It was the first time he had addressed her directly since the night before. She said a little hastily, 'It's built of rammed earth, which is why there are no creaks.'

'Really?' Mr Fairleigh was interested. 'I didn't realise there were very many buildings of that sort of construction in New Zealand. Obviously they last well. Do they need any special care?'

'Good roofing,' Leon said succinctly. 'And protection from the rain. If that's given, they'll last forever.' He stood up, instantly dominating the room. 'Mr Fairleigh, if it's possible, I'd like to speak to you.'

'Carl, my name's Carl.' He leapt to his feet, then looked a little helplessly at the children.

'Alexa will take care of them,' Leon said casually.

As the two men left the room Chris began to laugh. 'And that, my dear, is when you learn your true place in my big brother's life. Women are a convenience.'

Alexa composed her face into its usual mask. 'Nice to be told,' she said drily, leaning over to give Jodie a glass of orange juice.

He looked a little self-conscious. 'Well, hell, someone has to tell you. I must say, I'm disappointed in you. I thought you'd make him wait for a few more days.'

Arrested, hardly believing what she heard, Alexa lifted a brow and regarded him very steadily. If he could have, she thought he would have slid out of the room, but he assumed an expression of bravado she was beginning to recognise and ploughed on, 'Still, I should be used to that by now. What Leon wants, Leon gets.'

With that he did flee, leaving Alexa with a heart that felt as though the polar ice had moved in and taken over. It wasn't until a little voice said, 'Lexy?' that she came out of her profoundly humiliating reverie to see two pairs of eyes fixed on to her with enquiring looks.

'Well,' she said with a brightness only she knew was false, 'I think we'd better tidy up this table.'

The morning dragged on. She was 'helped' when she did the dishes and tidied up the already tidy rooms, then she armed herself with a box of the toys delivered by the shepherd's wife and used them to keep the children amused. No one came near them. At eleven o'clock she made a glass of orange juice for each of them and cut an apple into quarters, and at half-past twelve, warned by drooping eyelids and a tendency to whimper, she gave them sandwiches and took them up to her bedroom.

Her bed hadn't been made. She looked for a long moment at the rumpled sheets, then, her face set, pulled them up and popped each little body in. Within minutes both were sound asleep.

After watching the way their faces smoothed out in sleep she went across to the window and watched the sea. Wild and angry, the discoloured water clawed at the beach, the mountainous waves crashing in a lather of spray around the headlands. It was impossible to see the mainland through the spume and the showers of rain.

What was happening in the opposite bedroom? Was there anything she could do?

After some moments spent chewing her lip she left the children and knocked on the door. Raewyn's voice bade her enter.

Both she and the husband were in the room, but Alexa's eyes flew towards the woman in the bed. One glance told her that the baby was definitely on the way.

Raewyn said cheerfully, 'Ah, just the person Lois wants to see. Tell her how the children are, will you?'

'Asleep.' Alexa's glimmering smile seemed to reassure Lois. 'I've popped them down in my bed, and unless I'm needed here I thought I'd stay there with them so they don't wake up in a strange room by themselves.'

Lois Fairleigh smiled and nodded. 'That's kind of you. If they ask after me when they wake up, tell them I'm having a sleep. They're used to me resting a lot.'

Her face tightened, and Raewyn came forward, saying, 'Don't worry about them, they'll be fine. If Alexa can't manage them, Leon will. He's very good with children.'

'Good.'

Alexa felt the thankful glance sent her way and went out, closing the door behind her to the sound of a muffled little cry of pain.

The children were still asleep. She moved quietly around the room tidying it up, then sat down at the desk and began working once more on the paper she had started the day before.

Lost to the world, she sat in the uncertain light for almost two hours until Paul woke with a sobbing little cry and woke Jodie too. Both were inclined to be grumpy, but a wash of each shiny, flushed little face and a drink chased away the incipient bad temper. Once more, it was back to the morning-room and the box of toys.

When at last someone came in it was to see Alexa in the throes of an energetic game of 'Where's Paul?', ably abetted by Jodie and encouraged by Paul's charming baby laughter as he popped out from behind the sofa to their instant delight.

'Here Paul!' he crowed, as Alexa swooped on him and kissed his round little face.

'Me, too!' Jodie held hers up; Alexa picked them both up, pretended to stagger across to the sofa and collapsed on to it, holding them together in her arms, all laughing in the pretty room while the cyclone screamed outside.

Something, some atavistic instinct, lifted Alexa's head. Standing in the doorway was Leon, his strongly defined features drawn and taut as he watched them.

She asked faintly, 'Is—everything all right?'

He came into the room then, the strange mask-like expression fading into his normal smile. 'Yes, it's over. A little girl, and they're both well.'

Her breath hissed out through her lungs. She cuddled the children closer, smiling, her eyes blazing with joy and relief. 'I'm so glad,' she said softly.

He seemed startled, but after a second the familiar expression of mockery replaced that momentary soften-

ing. 'Really? Strange how all women react alike to the
news of childbirth, even those who show no signs of
wanting to become mothers themselves.'

He intended it to sting, and it did, but by now she
was an expert at hiding her feelings. Instead of reacting
she smiled at him with deliberate provocation, saying,
'Perhaps that's because it's women who actually have to
do the work. All men do is have their pleasure, then they
can walk away if they are so inclined. Women suffer the
pain and care for the results. They are more closely attuned to nature than men.'

His smile hardened. 'Well said. I might almost believe
you if it weren't for the fact that you are as finished and
polished a piece of artificial stone as any I've ever seen.
Would you have my child?'

She gaped, suddenly forced to face something she had
deliberately ignored since those abandoned hours in his
arms. But he misread her expression for he gave a sardonic smile and said, 'No, I thought not. I'm sure there's
no possibility of any result from last night's aberration.
You leave nothing to chance.'

'Lexy?' Jodie's voice was alarmed, her enormous eyes
fixed on to Leon's face.

He looked down at the two children, huddled like little
threatened animals in Alexa's hard grip, and the planes
and angles of his face softened miraculously. 'It's all
right,' he said gently. But when his eyes moved back to
Alexa's pale face they were cold as polished steel. 'You
and I have to talk,' he said. 'Later.'

Later turned out to be after dinner, in the office. Leon
was not in the least tactful. He said, 'Alexa, come with
me, please,' and when Chris looked up with a knowing
smile he stared stonily at him until it faded and there

was something like sympathy in the glance he sent to Alexa.

In the office he said politely, 'Sit down, please.'

She chose a hard upright chair, folding her hands primly in her lap like a schoolgirl. The room was warm and pleasant, but it didn't need the sound of the wind and the waves to chill her soul.

But once she was there he seemed hesitant, and when he spoke it was clear that he was choosing his words with care. 'Perhaps you would like to tell me what you intend to do now.'

'No.' The bald refusal startled her. She took a shallow breath and elaborated, 'I don't happen to consider it any of your business.'

'By sleeping with me last night you have made it my business.'

There was a prickle of tension between her shoulders. To rid herself of it, she shrugged. 'I don't see that at all.'

A fresh gust of wind shook the shutters, rattling them so that the sound rebounded weirdly in the room. In a voice totally free of inflections he said, 'I see. Then tell me why you allowed me to take you last night.'

'You didn't take me,' she said evenly. 'It was by mutual choice. If you are worried that I might presume on it, you can rest easy. I don't want any repetitions.'

He made a stifled noise and came across to stand in front of her. 'Look at me!' he commanded, that faint, foreign accent appearing once more in the deep voice. She obeyed, and saw him looming over her, tall and menacing in spite of the rigid control that she sensed was holding back emotions she couldn't recognise. Her lashes flickered, but she forced her stare to remain flat and impersonal.

'So it meant nothing to you.'

She shrugged again, taking a perverse pleasure in refusing to show her feelings. 'Of course it meant something,' she told him politely. 'It was a magnificent one-night stand. I'm sure I can't be the only woman to tell you that you're a wonderful lover.'

To her astonishment colour flowed across the arrogant cheekbones. He said between his teeth, 'Don't push too far!'

She felt the warning, and in her heart some small fetter of iron snapped. It was frightening, so she said harshly, 'What do you want me to say? That it meant all the world to me? Well, I'm sorry, I'm not going to oblige! It wouldn't have happened if it hadn't been for the cyclone, but it did, and I don't blame you. I'm not going to wail and cry. It's over, done, finished. You've made it more than clear that it meant nothing to you—if you've been upset by some old-fashioned idea that it is somehow vaguely shaming to sleep with a woman, then that's your problem, not mine. You have made it abundantly clear what you think of me. I am not going to plead with you to make an honest woman of me.' Her lip curled. 'I can live with myself. Perhaps my principles are a little more elastic than yours. Chastity is not for me the hallmark of a good character. Nor for you, I gather, otherwise you would have been a virgin last night.'

He was pale, the dark skin drawn tightly over the magnificent framework of his face. After a moment he said in a blighting voice, 'Very well, then. You have said enough.' He waited until she got to the door before asking, '*Is* there any possibility of a child?'

'I doubt it.' Even then, she couldn't lie to him.

'You will contact me if it happens.'

It was not a question, and when she maintained an obstinate silence she heard him sigh before he said, 'A child is—not a trifle, Alexa. I would wish to know if I made you pregnant.'

She almost laughed at that, but the hint of a threat in the cold tones stopped her cynical amusement. She said, 'All right.'

Then she went up to her bedroom. The children were asleep in her bed and she stayed looking down at them for a long time, her heart aching, before she climbed on to the truckle-bed she and Raewyn had made up. Outside, the wind showed no signs of abating. She listened to it for what seemed hours, and then she turned her face into the pillow and wept until her throat was as raw as her heart. After that, she lay awake remembering, until just before dawn when she fell asleep.

CHAPTER SEVEN

THE helicopter arrived as soon as it was light, but, early as it was, it hadn't beaten the children. Alexa had been up with them for an hour by the time the distinctive chop-chop-chop made itself heard above the wind and the rain, now at last no stronger than an ordinary storm.

They woke hungry, so she took them downstairs and was giving them breakfast when Chris came tearing in, rain running down his face, and said without preamble, 'You have to stay under cover. The bloody thing's full of reporters and Leon doesn't want them to know you're here.'

She bit her lip. He was right; she could think of nothing worse than facing journalists just now. Yet she hated the fact that through no fault of her own she was reduced to skulking like a crazed relation in corners and back rooms. She forgave Chris for the slight note of contempt in his voice, covering her feelings with a shrug.

The children looked up her, an identical expression of alarm on each small, sticky face. 'I'm going up to my room,' she said cheerfully, and kissed them before running lightly up the stairs. Even their enthusiastic embraces couldn't stop her from feeling smirched and dirty.

Once there she glanced out of the french windows across a sullen sea stained with silt, the waves still crashing heavily on to the beach. Clouds pressed down, their speed across the sky revealing a vigorous wind. The worst of the cyclone had passed, but there was still a sting in its tail.

No one came near her while she made the bed and tidied the room. It was difficult to hear what was going on in the rest of the house and she didn't dare look out the window in case some marauding reporter saw her. There were sounds in the passage outside, men's voices, Raewyn's giving instructions. Lois and the baby were being taken downstairs; Alexa stayed very still until the voices had died away.

She would have liked to see the baby, but Raewyn thought it was better for it not to be exposed to too many germs. Her heart contracted at the thought of a child of her own, someone to love and care for. Leon's child.

Firmly telling herself that she was suffering from the classic unloved child's syndrome, quite unfairly, because whatever her parents' faults she knew they loved her, she banished the idea. But not until she had sat down and worked out her cycle. No, it was highly unlikely that she was in any danger of pregnancy. And if she was—well, she would face that if it came.

The morning dragged. She sat down to work on equations but her heart wasn't in it. After making several mistakes that a schoolgirl would have scorned she pushed the paper listlessly away and sat with her head in her hand. The wind tossed the fronds of the palm trees unmercifully, shredding the long leaves into thin strips, whisking them from the ground high in the sky. There were no birds about, no sign of life. It would take months for the garden to recover from the battering.

And it would, she thought, driven by the empty morning to face her thoughts at last, take her months to recover from the effect of Leon Venetos in her life.

It didn't seem fair that, after waiting so long to fall in love, her wayward heart should choose a man like him, whose cynicism made a happy ending impossible. It helped to dwell on her sense of injury because that way she could almost overlook the frightening chill in the region of her heart, as though a large chunk of it had been stolen.

But of course she would get over it. Only an obsessed woman stayed in love with an unattainable man. Love needed to be reciprocated to live and flourish. And she was certainly not obsessive. It was probably going to be a miserable few months while she got over him, but get over him she would.

Firmly repressing the suspicion that she might be like her parents, who had never really been able to throw off the shackles of their fated marriage, she told herself that it was probably a good thing that she had fallen in love now, because a broken heart was guaranteed to take her mind off the mess she had made of her life.

A little suffering was par for the course. Everyone had to have a broken heart at least once in their life; it was part of the human condition.

It did not help to recall the overpowering sensuality of the night they had spent together. She told herself sturdily that of course he was an excellent lover, skilled and intuitive; heaven knew, if the newspapers were anything to go by he'd had enough practice. She should be glad that her initiation had been accomplished by a master, even if she had very little else to be glad of.

Self-pity had always been an emotion she despised, so she put it very firmly from her and occupied herself with wondering just what she was going to do with her life. She had come to the conclusion that the future she had always envisaged for herself, an academic career, was not what she wanted. She had enjoyed her life as a money manipulator, enjoyed pitting her wits against others, and the hunger to achieve. There were things she didn't enjoy, of course, but the years spent living close to the edge had spoiled her for the essentially enclosed world of the university.

Yet her future lay with her intuitive grasp of mathematics. Without boasting, she knew that she had an insight into the field granted to few. She needed to use it, to build on her strengths and grow with them. Frowning, she began to use some of the skills she had gained in her commercial training to plot some sort of scheme that would get her back on course.

The noise of the helicopter intruded into this. She watched as it swung over the house and headed back towards the mainland, the dull chop-chop-chop of the rotors fading at last into the sound of the wind and the waves. Her first instinct was to go downstairs, but she waited in case some reporters had stayed.

After about twenty minutes Raewyn slipped surreptitiously through the door. Looking anything but relaxed, she said softly, 'I'm sorry, but you'll have to stay here for at least another hour or so. Leon commandeered the chopper to take the Fairleighs back, so the place is still full of reporters. Well, two of them and a TV cameraman. Leon thinks it would be best if you stayed where you are until they're gone.'

'So do I,' Alexa said fervently.

The housekeeper relaxed. 'It seems awful to keep you hidden up here like a prisoner...'

Alexa managed a grin. 'Believe me, the alternative is equally awful. I have seen enough of journalists to last me all my life. I'll stay well out of sight until they're well and truly gone.' She hesitated, then asked, 'Has anyone been over to the bach? I haven't had time, and I wondered...'

'Leon went over. It's in a bit of a mess, I gather.' She looked sympathetic as Alexa's expression tightened. 'I'm sorry. I haven't had time to find out exactly what the damage is, but I heard him tell Chris that it looks as though a branch was flung through one of the windows, and the rain flooded across the floor in the sitting-room.'

Alexa nodded, chiding herself for feeling totally bereft. 'I expected as much,' she said evenly. 'It could have been worse.'

Raewyn looked relieved. 'Don't worry about it, Leon will see that it gets put into order.'

Not if I have anything to say about it, Alexa thought. The last thing she wanted was to be beholden to Leon Venetos any more than she already was. Shelter and succour from a cyclone was a neighbourly thing to do, but repairing her house was not. She would see to it herself.

'I'll get you some food up,' the housekeeper said. 'Really, these reporters!'

Which admirably summed up Alexa's view on the breed.

An hour later she was eyeing her tray with appreciation. There was soup, delectable pea and ham, a salad and hot chicken pie, and a large thermos of coffee to drink with the fruit and cheese and biscuits. Clearly Raewyn assumed her to have the appetite of a stevedore. Unless this was going to have to last through the rest of the day!

After the meal she curled up in the armchair with a volume of Trollope, losing herself for a few hours in the chronicles of that imaginary and wholly satisfactory county of Barsetshire; about, she thought once, as far removed from the aftermath of a cyclone twelve thousand miles away as anything could be, and all the more appreciated because of that.

The afternoon passed quickly, until at last she heard the helicopter again, and knew that her incarceration was almost at an end. Ten minutes later it was on its way, and within a few moments there came a knock at her door, and Chris's voice announced, 'You can come out now, Rapunzel.'

She was laughing as she came through the door, her blue eyes gleaming with amusement. He stared at her, and she could read a sudden comprehension in his regard, as though he was seeing her for the first time. He looked aware and self-conscious and very young.

'Have they all gone?' The question came hurriedly.

'Yes.' He followed her down the stairs, his self-possession restored. 'We had a couple of narrow shaves. The children wanted to say goodbye to 'Lexy' and we were terrified they were going to spill the beans, and one of the journalists saw Raewyn bring your lunch up, but we managed to convince him he'd seen her with an armful of towels rather than a tray covered by a cloth. Still, I'm glad to see them go.'

'So am I.' Alexa hid her smile. Clearly he had enjoyed the minor cloak and dagger aspect of the situation. It made him seem very young.

It was only four o'clock and the cloud cover was beginning to lift so that the light was brighter, more cheerful than it had been since the day before the storm struck.

Alexa felt like a prisoner released from long and onerous servitude. Her spirits soared, but her expression remained calm, almost rigid with control.

Leon watched her come down the stairs, his face carved in some dark wood. He wore a pair of dark trousers and a thin Italian shirt of fine pale blue cotton, and he looked stunning, all masculine vigour and potent male magnetism, the sandy fire of his hair lighting up the hallway.

Alexa felt as though she had been hit in the solar plexus. Her heart gave a violent lurch and unbidden, unwanted colour surged up through the delicate skin and gave its glow to her cheeks, heating the blue of her gaze to blazing azure. Perhaps then she realised that the pep talks she had given herself up in her bedroom had been whistling in the wind. She would never get over this man. Oh, she would probably learn to love again—even after failure, the human heart searches in hope—but she would never know that wild, sweet surrender, that rapturous certainty again.

Whatever happened, it would be worth it. It was rare and precious, a miraculous blending of passion and respect and admiration. She had, she thought in a moment of inspiration, been granted a great gift. It was up to her what she did with it.

'Raewyn said that the bach is damaged,' she said quickly, before that inscrutable gaze read too much in her face.

He nodded. 'Fortunately it's only a matter of replacing the glass and mopping up the floor. It's just the sitting-room; the rest of the place came through without any damage, and the pump and generator are both working.' He opened the door into the office, standing courteously back to let her precede him.

Once inside she said, 'I'll go on over, then.'

'Not yet. Wait until we've cleared it up.'

She looked out of the window and said swiftly, 'I'll go back and do it myself.'

'If you wish.' He was remotely courteous, his expression bland and impenetrable except for the keen scrutiny of his eyes. 'You don't have to go back.'

She sighed. 'Of course I do.'

'You could stay.'

Her mouth trembled. She fought a wave of longing so strong she thought it must be tangible. Then she said, 'No. Thank you—but the answer has to be no.'

If she had entertained a faint hope that he might ask her to stay, she was deluded. He looked at her with those hard eyes and that hard face, and he said, 'You are right, of course. I'll see that the place is made habitable.'

The breath she drew to speak was like knives in her throat. 'That's not necessary.'

He made no further objection. In fact, he didn't even come out when she left in the Range Rover with one of the men. Alexa told herself she was relieved.

Obviously under orders, the driver stayed, putting up a sheet of plywood to cover the broken pane while she cleared the glass from the floor. When that was done, and he had checked the electrical system and the pump to make sure they were still working, he handed over a box of provisions and a large basket provided by Raewyn, and went away.

Alexa went to bed and slept like the dead. In the morning the waves were still thumping heavily in, but the sun banished any gloom. Alexa took her breakfast out on to the terrace and ate it on the lounger. As well as the makings of a lettuce salad and half a cold roasted chicken, Raewyn's basket had provided fresh-baked bread and a bottle of milk. She ate without tasting it, then made her bed up and put the washing in the machine, thankful that the ceramic tiles and modern materials made cleaning up so simple.

All morning she worked steadily, mopping the mud and fragments of leaves from the floor, washing down the windows to rid them of their layers of salt. The water was still too discoloured to go for a swim, so after lunch she walked around the bay, marvelling at how little damage had been done. The pohutukawas were still intact, although there was a litter of leaves beneath them, and their blossoms had been entirely stripped by the wind but, apart from driftwood tossed way above the high-tide mark, there was little to show that only a couple of days before the wind and water had joined in a mad destructive partnership.

That night was not so easy. She lay awake, staring out of the window with tearless eyes as the aftermath of the cyclone faded and died, and she was left with the taste of humiliation in her mouth.

In the morning she woke, frowning, to the sound of an engine. At first she thought it was a helicopter, but after a few seconds it resolved into the thrum of a large launch, and from the sound of it above the still heavy thump of the waves, it was close in. Ignoring the brilliant sun, she rose quickly and pulled on some clothes, her frown deepening as she heard the steady hum become louder and louder, until it was clear that it was negotiating the rocks at the entrance to the bay.

By the time she had dressed and combed her hair the engines had been cut, and when she went out on to the terrace the boat was sitting quietly, an alien thing, in the middle of the bay. She caught the flash of glass and frowned again, wondering what the launch was doing there, and who was watching her through binoculars.

After a moment she went back inside and began to make her bed. A hard knot just above her stomach prevented her from eating the breakfast she knew she should have, but she made a cup of coffee. Drinking it helped lessen the prickle of unease that had wracked her since she heard the engines.

It was like being spied on. She hated it so much that when a small rubber dinghy left the side of the boat and roared up on to the beach she almost welcomed it.

Standing in the shade of the creeper on the terrace, she watched warily as a man got out and began to walk across the sand. It was the camera that warned her. Her first instinct was to whirl around and run, hide as far away as she could from the inquisitive, insensitive, prurient curiosity of the world. But she stood her ground, allowing him to what she deemed high-water mark. Then she called out, 'You're trespassing.'

He grinned, and kept coming. He was middle-aged and thin, his hair balding back on a tanned head, and he looked cheerful and friendly—and ruthless. 'Miss Severn, I'd like to talk to you.'

Her eyes looked right through him. 'You are trespassing,' she said, then turned away, walked into the house and pulled the curtains.

He didn't come in, but he didn't go away. Occasionally he called out to her. 'I just want to talk to you, Miss Severn, and then I'll go.'

Sometimes he asked her a question. 'How well do you know Leon Venetos? Did you know that Sam Darcy has left hospital? Word is that he's resigned. Are you in contact with him?'

And he walked around the house, making sure that she didn't escape him through the back.

She ignored everything, wishing only that he would go away and leave her alone. Yet in a way it was a relief to have him there because while she was fuming with anger and frustration she wasn't grieving for her own stupidity in falling in love with a man like Leon Venetos.

She never expected him to come. After that very definite rejection it didn't occur to her that he'd come to see how she was managing, although she should have known enough of his sense of responsibility to expect him. But the distinctive note of the Range Rover's engines filled her with shocked dismay. She wanted to run out of the bach and warn Leon away; she even headed for the back door, then stopped, her heart thumping in her chest, when she heard movement out there.

It was, she thought sardonically, like all the best horror stories.

However, she relaxed a little, because of course it wouldn't be Leon who came, he'd have sent someone else to make sure that she was all right.

She was wrong. Standing still in the hot stuffy sitting room she heard the reporter's friendly voice, and Leon's curt answer. In spite of the heat she shivered. There was a note of such cold, deadly ferocity in his voice that she was not surprised when the next thing she heard was the sound of the engine in the dinghy.

Her hands twisted in front of her. She waited tensely while the note of the dinghy's motor was replaced by the deep growl from the launch, then she drew a deep breath and went out around the back, where she was hidden by the biggest pohutukawa.

Leon was standing beneath it, his form almost impossible to pick out in the dense shade, and she knew from the way he stood that he was furious. Her heart thumped in her chest. So potent was the spell of his dark threat that she felt fear rise bitter as bile into her throat. He turned, although she had made no noise, and came back towards her, the sun gleaming fire-gold in his hair. Fair men are playboys, she thought inanely. They had no right to look powerful, arrogant and ruthlessly, uncompromisingly formidable.

He said harshly, 'What did you tell him?'

'That he was trespassing.'

'That's all?'

She gave a pale twisted smile. 'Whatever you think of me, Leon, you must be aware that I don't willingly talk to reporters.'

'Yet you must have. How else could he know you were here?'

The unfairness brought a fugitive colour into her cheeks. 'I don't know. Someone yesterday must have talked. Or the Fairleighs. I can assure you it wasn't me.'

Unforgivably, he said, 'You could have made some attempt to let me know that he was here. I don't want to figure in the gutter Press as your latest victim!'

'How?' Her composure cracked wide open. With eyes a blazing blue she spat the word at him, her cheeks flaming and her mouth drawn into a tight, fierce line. 'Just what did you expect me to do? Crawl out through the back window and run? He did patrols around the damned house, damn you! How the hell was I to know that you were going to come driving over? You made it

quite obvious that you didn't want to see me again—
you didn't...' She stopped precipitately, because she
wasn't going to reveal just how much his deliberate snub
had hurt.

'I didn't even see you off yesterday.' His smile was
narrow. 'I was busy. But you should have known, my
beautiful Alexa, that I'd have been over. Like your other
men, I've fallen under your spell. I need to sate myself
in you.'

'You must be joking.'

'Unfortunately, no. You possess a rare and distinctive
sensuality, an allure that promises more than it can deliver.' His eyes assessed her, coldly and deliberately, as
though she were in the block at a sale; she drew a deep,
horrified breath as he continued, 'But this time you are
going to deliver, Alexa. The odd thing is, I don't think
your former lovers have ever touched the depths in you.
You have a strange kind of innocence—perhaps it's the
innocence of prostitution, unawakened by desire.
Whatever it is, I want it. When I get rid of you, Alexa,
you'll know damned well what it is like to desire a man
so much that everything, all the cold, clever calculations
you've built your life on up until now, are swept away
by the sheer force of need—for one man, a man who is
offering you nothing beyond the sensual pleasure of the
moment. No power, no position, no money, only the
simple satisfaction of a need.'

His words terrified her. She shook her head, saying
in a shaking voice, 'What you are offering is degradation, and you know it!'

'Is it degrading to go to bed with a man just because
you want him?' He smiled. 'You have a strange sense
of values, Alexa.'

'It is degrading to lose everything in a flood of passion.' She tried to make him see, tried to hide the overwhelming pain caused by his implacable words. 'Where there is no respect, no affection, passion is just an animal coupling, impersonal and obscene. Leon——'

'Is that how it seemed to you?' His voice was level, almost light, totally at odds with the ferocity that looked out from his eyes. 'The coupling of two animals? There is something totally twisted about your values if you believe that selling yourself is somehow more worthy than giving yourself.'

He smiled, and she backed away, realising only now how he had misread her words. 'No,' she whispered. 'I didn't mean—no, Leon.'

'Shall I show you what the coupling of animals is like? Without respect, without affection? Just so that you have a comparison, you understand.'

She shook her head, backed up now against the wall. 'No, Leon,' she whispered, but the words were taken from her mouth, crushed into nothing by the predatory feral wildness of his.

He stripped her efficiently and without care, subduing her struggles with an effortless ease, until she was naked except for the brief scrap of cotton around her hips. And all the time that merciless mouth invaded hers, forcing her response, shaming her with the abandon of her response, until she was witless and shaking, her heart throbbing painfully in her chest.

Once she sobbed his name, and he lifted his head and smiled at her, a devil's smile, cold and without humour, a merciless movement of lips that knew every delicate curve and contour of her body. His eyes were black, shadowed by lust and anger; his hands gentle, yet ruthless. He did not hurt her. She was in agony.

When the tears came he took them into his mouth, so erotic a gesture that she sighed, allowing at last the tide of passion that his rough wooing had roused to flow forth without impediment.

Mindless, lost, she surrendered, her arms coming up to wind themselves around his shoulders, hold his big body close against her in a gesture that revealed the magnitude of her surrender.

He froze. And then he put her away, saying bleakly, 'So now you know. But you still want me, don't you, Alexa? Hell, isn't it?'

She watched him go with a black fury in her heart, and a great, unappeased need that ached through her like a mortal wound.

It was still there when she woke the next morning, it shadowed the whole day. By the time afternoon came she realised with despair that she had spent the morning waiting for Leon. Hating herself, hating him, she went for a walk through the paddocks to the spring, forcing herself to look about her with the nearest approximation she could find to keen interest. The island had come off comparatively lightly. There were several raw scars on the steeper hillsides, but apart from some scouring by floodwaters she couldn't see very much damage at all.

However, just beyond the spring, still turbulent and muddied, there was a small plantation of native trees, tiny saplings that had been battered by the down-draught along a gulley; wrenched by the cruel force of the wind, they were now at all angles, pathetic and forlorn. Alexa stared at them for a few minutes. Touched as she had been by Leon's desire to restore the island's cover, she could not bear to see the small valiant trees die. Without thought she made her way across to them and began to straighten the small saplings, easing them upright and pressing the earth around their roots with gentle hands. This she could do to help.

It was tiring work and her back and knee were feeling the effects of it by the time encroaching dusk brought her upright again. She groaned and pressed a hand into her waist, then stretched. Most of the small trees were now standing upright, eagerly setting roots into the warm damp soil. She smiled, thinking that the rest she could do tomorrow.

Leon came when she was standing on the terrace, watching the western sky. With its horns pointing to the north the new moon lay cradled in the last rays of the sun, a huge star gleaming like a promise of enchantment above it. Together they stood and watched until the last exquisite colour seeped away into the profound hush of the night.

Then he murmured, 'Venus, the evening star.'

Alexa nodded, wishing that it had been some other, less evocative planet than the one named for the goddess of physical love. Her lashes drooped, hiding the flare of hunger that lit her eyes to blazing cobalt. Leon was smiling, strong teeth white against the smooth tanned skin, the laughter lines adding emphasis to the virile beauty of his features.

He could be so charming, and then when her defences were down, he attacked like the swine he was. And she rather thought she might die if she didn't have him.

He said quietly, 'I'm sorry.'

'For what?'

'For behaving like a bastard.'

She shrugged. 'It doesn't matter.'

'I think it does.'

She could feel him just behind her, feel his presence with the pores of her skin, the nerves reacting to his male virility. The hairs on the back of her neck tightened. She said calmly, 'Don't worry about it.'

'Why? Because you expect me to behave with such a total lack of finesse? I damn near raped you—just to prove a point.'

She waited for him to tell her what the point was, but when he said nothing more she answered quietly, 'But you didn't.'

He laughed without humour. 'No, I had that much self-control.'

Without looking at him she said, 'It never occurred to me that you would rape me. I wasn't afraid.'

'I—I don't know that I deserve that tribute. Thank you.' Strangely he seemed shaken.

She flashed a quick look up at him and saw that his expression was not as unyielding as it normally was. He didn't look any softer—it was impossible to imagine Leon and softness together, but he did seem to be approachable as he had never been before. She didn't want to break the rapport that seemed to stretch so tenuously between them so she stood quietly, letting the peace of the night encompass them.

Above them, in the great sweep of the heavens, the coral sheen of sunset faded and died. Swift dusk settled over them and the thin pale crescent of the moon came to rest on top of the hills on the mainland. Stars pricked through, first small and faint, then more and more brilliant until the sky was a blaze of white light, hard, impersonal, breathtaking in its beauty.

He asked idly, 'Why did you resign from the bank, Alexa? Why did you run back here?'

For the first time she answered him without reservation. 'I couldn't stay. I couldn't work with Sam any more. And I owed it to the firm...the gossip was making it a laughing stock.'

He lifted his brows, assessing her with the keen scrutiny she had become accustomed to, but she could read his surprise and the disbelief that followed it. Hope, so brief a flower, died unborn. She would not try to explain her reasons to him because he was like all of the others, he wanted to believe only the salacious details.

Her profile rigid with a disappointment she refused to yield to, she stared stonily across the velvet waters of the bay.

'By resigning, you admitted that you were at fault,' he said, his voice deep and smooth and without expression.

She laughed, a hard little sound that made him frown. 'Now, Mr Billionaire, you know better than that.'

The beach lay before them, the sand still holding some of the glow of the sun. Quiet and still, the water was ruffled by the faintest breath of wind. Tiny waves sounded like the susurration of silk over pagan, gleaming limbs. Apart from that there was no sound, no movement. The beach, the sea, the dark expanse of the mainland were as silent and still as they must have been a thousand years ago, before the ancestors of the Maoris came down in their endless odyssey from their tropical homelands to this loneliest and most beautiful of all their landings.

Alexa felt her heart beat high in her throat. A pang of pleasure so exquisite it was allied to pain closed her eyes. She thought dizzily that she had been waiting all her life for this moment, this man, this place. And now it had come, and she could never experience it again, because she loved him and all he wanted from her was the temporary possession of her body.

'What are you planning to do now?' His voice was remote, as though some of the fey enchantment of the moment had touched him.

Alexa said quietly, 'I don't know. I came here to— for sanctuary, I suppose.' Her cynicism had vanished. It had never been a part of her character, merely a cloak she had assumed so that she wouldn't get hurt.

'Coming home,' he said, as though he understood.

She nodded. 'My mother was furious. She had been proud of me, and then all this blew up. She wanted me out of the way so that the scandal would die down more quickly.'

'And you ran.'

She responded to the note of condemnation with a huddled little movement of her shoulders, but then straightened up, holding them defiantly. 'So I ran. I thought it was the only thing I could do for Sam. Only to find that Sam had chosen his own way out.'

A note of raw emotion entered his voice, but he had mastered it before he'd said three words. 'He ran too.'

'Damn it, he was forced to,' she said fiercely. 'Everything he'd worked for, his whole life was going down the tubes, but he's strong, he'd have weathered that. It was when his wife started to——'

'For pity's sake! What the hell did you expect? That she'd just sit by while a high-priced courtesan made her and her husband a laughing stock across the front pages of the world?'

The sudden savage contempt made her flinch, but she retorted curtly. 'She was so stupid. If she'd used some common sense she'd have realised that for Sam it was just a temporary thing, a last snatch at youth. My mother called it a mid-life crisis. I honestly think that was what it was. We were never lovers.'

'Yes, I had noticed that it's some time since you've slept with anyone. However, making love does not necessarily involve what we did.' His voice was unbearably knowing, cynical. Alexa felt the breath of degradation touch her, and wondered uneasily just what sort of man he was. 'And betrayal does not necessarily involve making love. Sam's wife clearly felt betrayed, otherwise why would she scream to the newspapers?'

'I can't believe that she did.' She had thought that if she could convince him that she and Sam had never been lovers, all would be right. But it was still very wrong.

Angry and bewildered, she got to her feet as if she couldn't bear to sit still. The material of her skirt swished against her legs as she paced the length of the terrace and back again. 'She was great friends with the first gossip columnist, the one who broke the story. I assume it didn't occur to her that he'd splash her confidences all over the newspaper. She's the sort of woman who can't hold her tongue. And right from the start she resented me because she thought her son should have had my position.' That hard little laugh came back unbidden. 'Have you met him? A useless hunk of arrogance. Now he did his damnedest to get me into bed! But she knew, none better, that——'

'Alexa, don't lie, don't try to justify yourself.'

He sounded bleak, as though he understood what she was doing and was tired of it, tired of her protestations, worn out and wearied by them because he was never going to believe her. He was convinced that she and Sam had been lovers, emotionally if not physically. Period. Finish. The omnipotent Leon Venetos had made up his mind, and there was no appeal from that decision.

Shivering, she hugged her arms about her body. It had grown cool and the first dampness of the dew was icy against her skin. 'I think you'd better go home,' she muttered.

'Why? Because I don't like to hear you spouting the lies you've said so often that you almost believe them?'

She reacted to the sardonic words with fury, launching herself across the terrace in an access of frustration that turned her into a wildcat, all bared teeth and crooked claws, her hands uplifted to tear the smile from his face.

Catching her by the wrists, he laughed, and in one smooth, strong motion pulled her into the cage of his arms and kissed her protesting mouth until she moaned in surrender and capitulated to the fierce tides of desire surging through her bloodstream.

When at last he lifted his head she said huskily, 'I hate you.'

'I know. That's because you can't put anything across me. And because I make you forget that you have a brilliant brain and the scheming intelligence of a Machiavelli. For once in your career you've met someone who sees you for what you are, and you don't like it because you've always had the upper hand before.' He laughed again deep in his throat, a confident, totally arrogant sound with a note of excitement buried below the surface, and went on, 'And because you are no longer in control of that lovely, seductive body. When we kiss it burns the stars out of the sky. And you hate that, too.'

She leaned her forehead on to his chest, listening to the thunder of his heart. Slowly she turned her face so that the warmth of him heated her cheek. He smelled of warm male, erotic yet safe, which was strange because he was the most dangerous man she had ever met.

His arms loosened their fierce grip. He eased her into a more comfortable position and rested his cheek on the silky top of her head. They stood like that for a long time, until she stepped out of his grip and said sadly, 'I'm sorry.'

'Are you?' His smile didn't soften his face. 'Alexa, I would like it if you told me the truth.'

She knew what he wanted. He was sexually possessive, but his possessiveness extended even further than that. He wanted a kind of emotional subjugation; her surrender. He demanded more of her than he was prepared to give himself, and that was why she couldn't give in to him.

She wouldn't take the easy way out. Desire for him was eating at her bones, but as well, she loved him... More than anything in her life she longed to say the words he wanted to hear, words of surrender and yielding, then go with him and rediscover the delights that he promised with every kiss, every movement of his lean, powerful body.

She couldn't do it, because she needed to know that he trusted her. Against all appearances, if necessary. If he didn't, then he considered her to be just another woman like all the others he had wanted and bedded over the years. A mistress, easily bought, as easily disposed of. She was playing for high stakes. Nothing less than some sort of acknowledgement from him that this wasn't just another affair.

Reason, common sense, told her that she was taking on a cause lost before it had begun. Who was she, Alexa Severn, to think that a man like Leon Venetos could give up his life as one of the most eligible bachelors in the world for her, a woman he suspected of selling herself to further her rapacious ambition?

But the logic her brain understood so well was not proof against the hidden intuition of an older part of her mind. He might never love her as she understood love, but he felt more than he had ever felt for any of the women he had taken and forgotten, because he wanted her to tell him the truth.

It was just unfortunate that when she did he didn't believe her. And short of actually giving in, surrendering her autonomy to his jealous demands, she didn't know how she was going to convince him that she had not prostituted herself to claw her way up the corporate ladder.

Stalemate.

'I have,' she said, fighting down a spear-thrust of pain. She began to walk across the short tufty grass towards the beach.

'Damn you!' His hand on her shoulder was hard and hurtful. She was whirled around and shaken. 'Don't you turn your back on me! All you have to do,' he said between his teeth, 'is tell me. There'll be no recriminations. I just want the truth from you!'

CHAPTER EIGHT

SHE demanded heatedly, 'Why is it so difficult for you
to believe that Sam and I were not lovers, that I was not
emotionally attached to him in any way beyond that of—
of father and daughter? You're testing me, making con-
ditions. Why? Why is it so important? Do you demand
a potted biography—with emphasis on the love affairs—
from all your other lovers? Because there's an unpleasant name for the sort of man who does that.'

His hands loosened. As he stepped back she said
boldly, 'After all, you don't want to marry me, do you?'

And waited with painfully held breath for his answer.
It came quickly, without pause for thought. 'Hell, no!'

Something inside her withered and died.

Before she had time to feel the pain he said curtly, 'Is
that why you won't give in? If you're holding out for
marriage, my dear, forget it. I don't like being
manipulated.'

'And I,' she said from the depths of a pain so intense
that she thought she might die of it, 'would refuse to
marry a man who thinks so poorly of me as you do.'

He smiled between his teeth. 'Then it's just as well
that you are such perfect mistress material, isn't it?'

His mouth was cruel, totally without respect, plun-
dering the sweet depths of hers with a ferocity that only
slowly gentled into passion. After a long moment he
lifted his head and stared down at her face, his own
shuttered and bleak. 'I don't believe that you and Sam

169

had a pure and platonic relationship because I doubt very much whether any man, unless he was in a wheel-chair, could look into those beautiful eyes and not im-agine himself master of that superb body. And you must have known what you were doing to him. So why didn't you put a stop to it?'

Her anguished, choking little gasp faded into a moan as his hand slid slowly from her throat to her breast, palming with deliberate sexuality the sensitive tip. Heat raced from the pit of her stomach, and every nerve jerked with the presence of danger. His eyes were black, smouldering like dark embers, and the strong features were taut with an unbearable tension.

'You are so beautiful,' he said softly. 'A man could lose his soul in those eyes, in this body, so that when he thinks he is at his most powerful, the conqueror of all that he wants, he loses all that is important: his honour, his strength, his very manhood. You promise so much— to deliver the pleasures of paradise. And when we lay together, that promise was more than fulfilled. So sweet and fiery and abandoned, with your throaty voice and your sinuous body that fits so tightly around me, those gasping little sounds when we both went over the top together... Dead sea fruit, beautiful to look at but filled with ashes, Alexa, because you refuse to allow anyone into your heart, your mind, anywhere near the person who hides behind that exquisite body and face.'

The mesmeric note in his voice didn't sweeten the bitter words. Alexa shook her head, blinking, and saw his total rejection, his refusal to accept her in any other role than that in which he had cast her. And in that moment she saw his arrogant determination to make her his mistress, his toy. He despised her, but he was prepared to ignore that because he wanted her.

Fear drove her to wrench away, but he laughed deep in his throat and pulled her back into the frightening haven of his arms.

'No,' she said carefully.

'Why not? We're magic together.'

But she was shaking her head, trying very hard to keep calm; he had, she realised, lost control. Speaking in as soothing a voice as she could, she said, 'It's not enough, Leon.'

'I know it's not enough, but it's going to be all that we can have. I despise you, but I despise myself for wanting you even more.' His features hardened on to granite as his hands tightened on her shoulders. 'Lust, my most delectable Alexa, is an ugly response to beauty, superficial and callow, but when it's a reaction to shallowness, it's excusable. And you won't give me anything more than the easy response of your body to mine. So be it. I'll take it.'

Truly frightened she said quietly, 'No.'

His mouth curved in a mirthless smile. 'You don't mean it.'

She did, but he kissed her with such poignant sweetness that she was lost. And when he drew her down on to the lounger she went willingly, even though her heart was weeping. This time it was slow, exquisitely, agonisingly slow. Oh, the fire was there, and the mindless intensity, the glowing, seething sensuality, but this time there was grace and appreciation, the skilful pleasuring of a man who knew how to wring the utmost response from a female body.

When at last they lay gasping together the kindly night was all around them, fragrant with the scent of growing things and the exotic flavour of the sea, sounding like the background to all dreams.

Salt air, and salt in her mouth; she touched her tongue to his shoulder, tasting the sweat that dried there. And his instant response, the shivering of the tiny muscles beneath the oiled silk of his skin, the shifting and flexing of the larger muscle, brought the sting of salt to her eyes.

She said nothing, but when he at last rose and pulled her to her feet, her eyes were huge and luminous in her face and he kissed them closed. 'I won't suggest you come back to the homestead,' he said matter-of-factly, 'otherwise I'll never get any work done. But I'll come whenever I have time.'

He couldn't have put her position in his life in a more insulting way. Humiliation robbed her of speech, but only for a moment. In a voice that was hard and indifferent she told him, 'I won't be here. I'm leaving.'

'How?'

She averted her face when he turned away and began to pull his clothes on, taking his time. When she gave no answer he straightened up and, without looking at her, said, 'You were the one who wanted to come here so much that you promised Sean your favours if he'd get you here. But he knows he'll lose his job if he takes you back, so even if he was stupid enough to fall for the same trick again, it won't get you off the island.'

Alexa's jaw dropped. 'What? Did he tell you that?'

'He did. Bewailing the fact that he should have known that you'd renege on the deal once he got you here.'

A black fury drove her around in front of him so that he couldn't shoulder into the shirt in his hands. 'Just you listen to me,' she ground out through gritted teeth. 'I did not promise him anything, and before I leave this place he's going to admit it. I'll——'

'You'll do nothing!' The words whipped through the cool air. 'Don't even bother to lie. If you hadn't promised to sleep with him, why weren't you out for his blood? I'm sure that if he had tried to rape you, as you claim, you'd have wanted him off the island. Yet you weren't particularly surprised to see him again, and you certainly didn't flinch away or greet him with any sort of loathing.'

She whispered in a harsh, impeded voice, 'I thought he'd lost his head! Damn it, he *had* lost his head! He wouldn't have raped me—and even if he did try it, I could disable him in about fifteen different ways! It never occurred to me that the little weasel would try to save his bacon by lying to you. How dare he? And how dare you?'

He laughed and finished dressing, ignoring her temper. Then he came over and kissed her hard, holding her mutinous face still while he looked down into it. 'So we'll have no more about you leaving,' he said deliberately. 'As long as I want you, you'll stay. And when you do leave, it will be because I no longer want you.'

She lit a fire on the point the next morning, and when a family launch came in close, she capered and danced by it until they sent in a dinghy to see what was happening. By evening she was back in Auckland, exhausted and so sunk in pain that she wanted nothing more than to weep for a week. The only thing that gave her any cause for pride in her behaviour was the scathing note she had left for Leon.

Thank heavens Cathy and Jake were home, sympathetic and very dear, deducing that now was not the time to ask questions. Instead, Jake went about his writing, wrestling with a play, while Cathy spent a lot of time catching up with the convolutions of the Durrant Trust, an enormous foundation she had set up to deal with the problems of children in need. They were concerned, but silently supportive, and Alexa slowly began to relax. She spent a lot of her time working on her equations, because that was the only time she could forget Leon. She even sent out feelers to see if there was any possibility of a job at the university.

Then, one night, Leon appeared on television. He was leaving New Zealand for Zurich and wouldn't be back for some months, and after Alexa watched him in white-faced misery, Cathy came into her bedroom and said in her blunt way, 'OK, spill the beans. You've been so matter-of-fact that it is obvious you're in deeper trouble than that London business. Who is the man?'

'Most people think it was Sam Darcy.'

Cathy snorted. 'I know you better than that.'

So Alexa told her. Cathy sighed. 'The fabulous Leon? Well, I must say, when you fall, you choose the highest cliff...'

'Do you know him?' Alexa shouldn't have been surprised, for Cathy had grown up in the circles that Leon had made his own.

'Yep. Gorgeous. One of the few men I've ever looked at apart from Jake. But definitely not for beginners.' She frowned for a few seconds, then cheered up. 'Still, neither was Jake.'

Alexa nodded. It was all very easy for Cathy to be a little complacent at her success in taming such a moody, brilliant man as Jake, but Cathy had charisma, a kind of sultry beauty that was as alluring as it was impossible to forget or qualify.

Alexa had no illusions about her own looks. They were all very well, but without that necessary mystery. She was not special. Open any magazine and there were pages of women as good-looking as she, if not better.

'Feel like telling all?'

She sighed. 'Not a lot to say. He thinks I barter myself in various unmentionable ways for power and advancement. He refuses to be another pathway to the golden handshake for me, unless it's the one he gives to all his mistresses.'

Cathy's eyes widened. 'And how does he know all this?'

'Like everyone else, he reads the papers.'

'Of all people, he should know that newspapers can be long on insinuation and speculation, short on facts. And what does he mean by unmentionable ways?'

Without thought Alexa said, 'I don't know. He's the expert, not me.'

Cathy grinned at the flood of colour that swept through her pale skin. 'Were you still a virgin? I somehow thought you were. I'll bet it was just as much a shock for him as it was for Jake, when we—well, then! But at least he never came up with "unmentionable ways"! And I'll bet Leon Venetos doesn't really believe that, either. You know what it sounds like to me? I think the man is hooked, and he's desperately looking for an out—any out, even if it's ridiculous.'

'And why should he do that?'

Cathy shrugged. 'Oh, these men—they're conditioned to think that they are so strong and tough, that it's somehow a weakness to admit to needing a woman. His father was Italian, too, wasn't he? Macho, men of his generation were.'

Alexa said slowly. 'I don't think that's it. He's not some fool, so hooked on his idea of masculinity that he can't see how blind he is. And I suppose he did have reason.'

At Cathy's questioning glance she told her about Sean, and the excuse he had used.

Cathy snorted again. 'That's just the usual weak excuse men have made, from Adam on. It wasn't my fault, the woman did it. I don't think that Leon Venetos would believe him unless he wanted to. Poor Alex, you must have been scared out of your mind! What swines men are!'

'Not really. Sean wouldn't have raped me.' Her mouth twisted. 'He'd been reading the papers too, and he thought I'd be eager for any man.'

Cathy's answer to that was a selection of syllables she said was an Inca curse. Alexa laughed, feeling a warmth invade the frozen regions of her heart.

'And the fact that I slept with Leon so soon after I'd met him just confirmed all his suspicions,' she said, confessing all. 'I was not one of those virgins whose condition makes their state apparent.'

'In other words, he couldn't tell. Happens to the best of us,' Cathy said, with airy insouciance. She got up and put her arms around Alexa, hugging her tightly. 'So you've gone and fallen in love with the man, because I know you, there's no way you'd sleep with him unless you really were in love. You and I, we're not the sort who finds it easy to overcome the inhibitions of our childhood. We don't fall in love—or in lust—easily, and when we do, we fall hard. Well, what are you going to do about it?'

'Nothing. I'll get over it.' At Cathy's disbelief she said, 'I'll have to.'

'If you just *want* Leon the Magnificent, you'll definitely get over it. It's not quite so simple when it's love. But it can happen.'

She didn't sound sure, though. And as the days passed, and the pain stayed raw and lacerating, Alexa began to wonder if she was ever going to recover.

In a way it was easier with him out of the country. It put a stop to wondering whether she was going to meet him on the street whenever she went out.

She published a paper in an esoteric magazine, and found herself a job in the office of an accountant who clearly had no idea who she was. The work was interesting, but it left her with plenty of time to think. She began to rent time on the university computer, and lost herself in her work. It was interesting and, because she used the computer at night, it took up the time when she couldn't sleep. Despite Cathy's heartfelt objections she moved into a rather seedy flat in one of Auckland's featureless western suburbs.

She was not pregnant. Sometimes she thought that she wasn't very human, either. Summer faded into a splendid autumn, warm and crisp and clear, and winter came, with rain and wind. The weather had never affected her moods before, but she found herself subject to rather vicious swings, up in the sky, then days of depression when it seemed that the sun would never shine for her again.

'You've got thin,' Cathy said anxiously.

'I've lost a little bit of weight. That's all.'

'Damn the man. Pride isn't worth anything. Why don't you contact him?'

'Because he doesn't want me.'

Cathy stirred her peppermint tea and sighed, her brilliant red head propped up on a slender hand. 'I thought Jake didn't want me, except in the most basic way, either.'

Alexa laughed. 'You had only to look at you two to know that you were in love!'

'Well, I didn't see it. He had to almost drown before I realised just how I felt. Why don't you contact Leon Venetos, Alex? How can he find you if he doesn't know where you are?'

She shook her head, the thick black mass swinging across to hide her face. Persuasively, Cathy urged, 'At least go up to the island so that he knows you're around.'

Alexa shook her head, but through that long winter the idea stayed maddeningly in her brain. She worked hard on her theories, following a tortuous path through philosophy and pure mathematics, physics and some ideas so speculative that they were still almost conjecture. It was exciting, immensely satisfying, and she should have been ecstatic when she was contacted by a very erudite and famous man of science in Britain who had read her article and thought they might be able to work together. She wrote back, half agreeing to go and see him, and thought wistfully of losing herself in England.

She pined.

So in Labour Weekend at the end of October she flew up to the nearest airport and hired a car. From Hogarth

Tom Hoskings in his water-taxi dropped her off, promising faithfully to return at midday on Monday.

It was like coming home. The island was green and lush, the house tidy and clean. The window, she noted, had been repaired. Making a mental note to repay him, she ate lunch then walked over to the small plantation of native saplings, and was delighted to find that they had all survived the cyclone and the winter.

He came after dinner, when the sky was green and a lovelorn *tui* sang and chuckled in the flame tree behind the bach.

He walked, so she didn't know he was there until her skin recognised him. She was lying in a chair on the terrace, her hands loosely curled in the lap of her white trousers as she watched the waves come in and out over sand the colour of his hair. Her face was pensive, but when the first tendrils of recognition began to prickle across her skin, it froze to impassivity, the smooth skin held tight by sheer will.

He said, 'Alexa,' and walked out of the shadows and on to the terrace, moving smoothly as a panther, graceful and powerful.

Her heart leapt in her throat, blocking out the sound of the sea. In her lap her hands trembled until she had to clasp them tightly together.

He said deeply, 'I began to think I was going to have to come and get you.'

'You didn't know where I was.'

'I did. I had you watched.'

Tears blurred her sight. 'Why?'

'Because I couldn't bear to lose you.'

'Then why didn't you come for me? It's been a long winter.'

'I know. But the decision had to be yours. I'd made so many mistakes—I couldn't afford to make any more.' His mouth twisted as he sat down on the lounger and took her hands in his warm strong clasp. 'I wasn't going to be able to last out much longer, though. If you hadn't come up this weekend I was going to come and get you. I'm not a patient man.'

She was afraid to believe what he was saying. In a cool remote little voice she asked, 'Why were you coming to get me? Lovers are two a penny, when you're a billionaire.'

The jibe made him frown, but he ignored it, saying with apparent irrelevance, 'I went to see Sam Darcy.'

In a strangely dissociated voice Alexa asked, 'How is he?'

'A chastened man.' He slanted her a mocking glance. 'Recovering, and feeling a fool.'

She smiled, the cynicism that had come so swiftly and shockingly in her life very evident. 'I told you he would. I'm glad he's over it.'

He shrugged. 'He's divorcing his wife.'

Alexa's breath hissed out on a sigh. 'I'm sorry to hear that, although I'm not surprised. What does surprise me is that she didn't beat him to the gun.'

'She knows which side her bread is buttered on. Besides, she had no cause, did she? You can't divorce a man for falling in love with another woman, when that's all that happened.'

It took a moment for the comment, delivered in a cool impersonal voice, to register. When it did she was surprised at the wariness that was all she felt. Too many times she had hoped, and had her hopes dashed. So she said, in a tone that matched his, 'Do I deduce that you are now convinced that he and I were never—never lovers?'

'I owe you that, I suppose.' But he didn't go any further, and she didn't like to push him.

The silence stretched unbearably before he turned his head to scan her downcast face, her shadowed eyes. 'Right from the first I didn't want to believe that you were lovers. It took me until the night of the cyclone to admit that it didn't really matter how many men had had that altogether too desirable body, as long as I was the last. That night when we made love, it was so patently novel for you that I was forced to face the fact that you could well be a virgin. However, I refused to face the implications. I told myself that that was probably part of your stock in trade, a talent for virginity so that each man who lost himself in you thought he was the first.'

Her shocked, wordless protest made him smile, a dangerous, feral movement of his lips that stopped any further comment. 'A very *useful* talent for a woman who considers her body to be a tool in her career. So I ignored the small instinct that told me I was wrong, that you and I had found something incredible, beautiful and rare and sweet as the waters of paradise, and decided that I'd been right when I decided that you would be a distinct acquisition as a mistress. Only you refused to fit the slot. You wouldn't stay with me, you made it more than obvious that although I could get you into bed it would be rape, mentally if not physically. And you frustrated the hell out of me. Which in part explains why I was so bloody brutal to you.'

'Yes,' she said in a small voice, remembering just how brutal he had been.

He took her hand and kissed it. 'I don't think I'm ever going to be able to forgive myself for that. I have no excuse—or at least the only one I can offer is probably worse than no excuse at all.'

'Perhaps I should hear it, nevertheless,' she suggested, wincing with a fierce repressed delight as he bit the soft flesh at the base of her thumb.

'I was fighting myself, not you. I think I'd recognised that whatever I felt for you was not going to be content with an affair and then a pay-off.' He laughed again, a derisory sound that made her fingers clench. He let her pull her hand away, his eyes darkening with something she didn't recognise, something that chilled her.

'You'd got under my skin. You were part of me, as essential to me as my blood and my breath. I had started off by wanting you with a jealous intensity that scared the hell out of me. Taking you should have quenched that. But it didn't. To my horror I at last realised that I needed you. And I have never needed a woman in my life. I felt—as though I had become a lesser man. It was unbearable.'

'I understand,' she said quietly. 'Much the same was happening to me. I grew up believing that being independent was the only way to keep from getting hurt, and then you stripped my independence away and I was a slave to emotions and sensations I had always feared. That was why I was desperate to get away. I just couldn't see beyond the pain of your inevitable rejection of me.'

He said gently, 'We were both fools.'

'Yes.'

The sun beat down on the drowsy air. It felt almost as warm as summer, yet there was a difference in the atmosphere; it was obviously spring.

In a shaken voice he said, 'Dare I ask for forgiveness, Alexa?'

At last she permitted herself to look fully at him. What she saw in the strong lines of his face made her heart turn over. For he was watching her with a naked pleading, his eyes devouring her as though she was his one hope of salvation.

'I'd forgive you anything,' she said.

He attempted to smile. 'I wouldn't want you to. You wouldn't be my Alexa if you lost your integrity. But I'll take that as a declaration of love.'

She laughed, and leaned over and kissed his shoulder. 'Am I to get one?'

'Oh, I think so,' he said, turning to her and taking her into his arms. He looked deep into her eyes, and that was his declaration, she had no need of words, for that long, solemn communion promised all that he was, all that he ever would be. But he gave her the words too, whispering, 'I love you so much, my beautiful grave Alexa, that I think you've driven me out of my mind. I've been behaving like a fool. Give me back my brain and you can keep my heart. It's not much good without you, anyway.'

'Oh—Leon!' Sudden tears drenched her eyes, but she didn't try to hide them. It was the work of a moment to fit herself into his arms as though she had never been away from them. Her mouth touched his, softly, eagerly, and was crushed open. When she could speak she said, 'I love you. I love you more than you'll ever know. More than I can ever tell you. Oh, damn this mathematical brain of mine! I wish I were a poet, so that I could find the words...'

He laughed. 'Instead of seeing love as $x + x =$ what? $2x$?'

'Oh, no.' She touched his mouth, and the strong line of his jaw, and the high aristocratic sweep of his cheekbones, delighted yet awed when he shuddered under her touch. '$x + x$ equals infinity,' she said softly. 'Forever.'

'So you see, you don't need to be a poet, maths is every bit as suitable for the job.' He laughed into her eyes. 'I wonder what sort of children we'll have, you and I? A mathematical genius for a mother, and a pirate for a father!'

'Whatever they are, we'll love them, won't we?'

He understood as he always had, and kissed her swift and hard. 'Yes, we'll love them.'

She said in a puzzled voice, 'I used to think that I could never allow myself to love anyone, that it was a kind of death. Now, I think I might love the whole world.'

'Really?' His brows lifted in that half-mocking, half-cynical movement she had grown to know so well. 'I think perhaps you should be happy with loving just me for the time being. Alexa, where do you want to marry? Shall we ask your mother to organise a wedding, or shall we go and marry quietly here?'

'I don't want my mother to have anything to do with it. She'll want a big wedding, and I want just us.' She spoke fiercely, afraid of the inevitable gossip, the acid comments in the newspapers, the conjecture and malice and degradation of the whole circus.

'Then we'll marry here. There'll be a fair amount of speculation; will you be able to deal with that?'

She laughed and stretched voluptuously, delighting in the instant response of the lean body so close to hers.

'I'll be with you,' she said simply. 'I can deal with anything.'

'I know how you feel.' Slowly, sensuously, he pushed her back on to the warm, dry grass. 'As though you could fly without wings. So—from this moment on, my dearest heart, you and I are husband and wife. I think perhaps we have been married since we saw each other. When I saw you in Sean's arms I wanted to kill him, because he was kissing my woman. I know I haven't wanted another woman since then. It is as simple and as complex as that.'

She laughed, prisoner of rising excitement yet refusing to surrender to it. 'So you behaved as badly as you could!'

'Because I knew that if you were mine, I was yours. My mind fought my heart, and my body knew only that without you it was not complete. Now, my beloved, I know that you are mine and I am yours, and I am whole again. So kiss me.'

She kissed him, and kissed him again, and shuddered under his searching, experienced hands, the heated, muttered words that came from his tongue. With a slow, inevitable beauty he stripped her of her clothes until she was lying naked in his arms, her eyes half-closed, an expression of such joy on her face that it seemed to blaze forth in a wild pagan beauty. His mouth touched her lips, her throat, the silken expanse of shoulder and neck, coming at last to the soft pink aureole that surmounted her breast. Her breath was swift and harsh in her throat; she wanted more than anything to hold his head to her breast, keep him there and feel the strong suckle of his mouth, but she was shaking, her body heated and unmanageable.

When he opened his mouth on to her she cried out, and a spasm of sensation, piercing and honeysweet, speared through her body. Her back arched; she said his name, and he brought up his hand to cup the soft high breast and began a dizzying, sensual massage.

'Leon,' she whispered. 'I don't know what to do.'

His breath was warm on her skin, an erotic little caress that made her shiver. 'What do you want to do?'

'I want—I want you.' Her hands pulled at his shirt, then got a purchase and ripped the buttons open. 'I love you,' she said fiercely, running her hands across the smooth steely warmth of his shoulders, her delight in being able to touch him written vividly in her face.

'My own private nymph, naked just for me,' he said, teasing her, his eyes narrowed to slivers of molten grey as they watched the contrast of her long, slender fingers against the deep Mediterranean tan of his chest. 'I've discovered that I have a very vivid imagination. I have indulged in more fantasies since I met you than ever before in my life.'

'Tell me.'

But he laughed deep in his throat and shook his head. 'Why bother with fantasies when I possess the real thing? Fantasies are for the starving; I have you now, my love, my treasure, my garden of all delights. Alexa...!'

She had run her hands down the strong chest and across the hard muscles at his diaphragm; her fingertips tingled and she felt his heart pick up speed. It gave her the courage to pull at the belt of his trousers, and slide her hand beneath the waistband.

The muscles across his stomach were a hard wall but they contracted in a spasm that made her snatch her invading hand away. Colour scorched across her cheeks.

She looked up, afraid that she would see something like contempt at her forwardness in his expression. Instead there was hunger, a primeval intensity that wiped the teasing lightness from his eyes and voice, leaving his face stripped and desperate, the hard bones clenched.

He groaned and kissed the spot where her heart threatened to burst and turned his head to lay it sweetly against her breast. 'I'm afraid I'll hurt you,' he said in a low voice.

'You couldn't.'

'Oh, lord, when you finally decide to trust, you make a good job, don't you? Alexa, I'll hurt you, it's part of the human condition. I'm not a superman, all-knowing, all-wise. Occasionally I'll let you down, and you'll hate me, and I'm terrified that you'll go...'

'For someone so clever, you are very stupid,' she said lovingly. 'We'll fight and we'll make up, and we'll enjoy both, because we love each other. I don't expect you to be superhuman. I'm an all too fallible human being, I couldn't live with someone who didn't make mistakes. But I love you, Leon. That's all that matters, isn't it?'

His arms tightened around her in a bone-crushing grip. After a moment he said softly, 'Yes, my dearest, that's all that matters.'

'Then,' she said, half laughing, wholly demanding, 'will you please get over your attack of nobility, or nerves, or whatever it is, and make love to me?'

His mouth quirked. 'Oh, yes,' he drawled. 'I can do that. Now—and for the rest of our lives together!'

Coming Next Month

Available in June wherever paperback books are sold, or through
Harlequin Reader Service:

In the U.S.
901 Fuhrmann Blvd.
P.O. Box 1397
Buffalo, N.Y. 14240-1397

In Canada
P.O. Box 603
Fort Erie, Ontario
L2A 5X3

Have You Ever Wondered If You Could Write A Harlequin Novel?

Here's great news—Harlequin is offering a series of cassette tapes to help you do just that. Written by Harlequin editors, these tapes give practical advice on how to make your characters—and your story— come alive. There's a tape for each contemporary romance series Harlequin publishes.

Mail order only

All sales final

Indulge a Little
Give a Lot

A LITTLE SELF-INDULGENCE CAN DO
A WORLD OF GOOD!

Last fall readers indulged themselves with fine romance and free gifts during the Harlequin®/Silhouette® "Indulge A Little—Give A Lot" promotion. For every specially marked book purchased, 5¢ was donated by Harlequin/Silhouette to Big Brothers/Big Sisters Programs and Services in the United States and Canada. We are pleased to announce that your participation in this unique promotion resulted in a total contribution of *$100,000.*

*

Watch for details on Harlequin® and Silhouette®'s next exciting promotion in September.

THE LOVES OF A CENTURY...

Join American Romance in a nostalgic look back at the Twentieth Century—at the lives and loves of American men and women from the turn-of-the-century to the dawn of the year 2000.

Journey through the decades from the dance halls of the 1900s to the discos of the seventies ... from Glenn Miller to the Beatles ... from Valentino to Newman ... from corset to miniskirt ... from beau to Significant Other.

Relive the moments ... recapture the memories.

Look for the CENTURY OF AMERICAN ROMANCE series starting next month in Harlequin American Romance. In one of the four American Romance titles appearing each month, for the next twelve months, we'll take you back to a decade of the Twentieth Century, where you'll relive the years and rekindle the romance of days gone by.

Don't miss a day of the CENTURY OF AMERICAN ROMANCE.

The women...the men... the passions...
the memories....

CARM-1